DECEMBER STORM

BOOK 3 OF THE FROST WITCH SAGA

BONNIE ELIZABETH

MY BIG FAT ORANGE CAT PUBLISHING

December Snow
My Big Fat Orange Cat
Urban Fantasy November 2020

My Big Fat Orange Cat Publishing
MyBigFatOrangeCat.com

ISBN: 978-1-953363-03-9 Trade Paperback

Most people would be overjoyed to see snow this close to Christmas, particularly in Central Kentucky where snow didn't fall often. Courtney sat on the too-soft sofa, sinking further down than she expected—something that happened no matter how often she plopped down—and looked at the tabletop Christmas tree without really seeing it. The second-floor room everyone called the library smelled of old books and cat urine.

Courtney tracked the falling white flakes as carefully as a hawk tracked a rat. The snow had started about an hour earlier and now fell quickly and silently through the gray sky. Her prediction on the arrival of the latest storm had been off by forty minutes.

From the room below, Courtney heard people talking, though she couldn't make out the words. She could have if she wanted to listen harder. The creature inside her wanted to reach out and feast on the emotions that were coming up. Worry and fear.

On the far side of the room, where Courtney was unable

to see her, Riley worked her way through piles of books in hopes of finding a way to rid Courtney of the creature that tried to possess her. For now, Courtney had a hold on the thing and kept it at bay.

A calico cat curled beneath the little tree with its handful of ornaments. The oranges and blacks and whites and even a patch of gray on a hind foot were in stark contrast to the plain green tree skirt that covered the bookshelf upon which the cat and tree sat.

The bookshelf sat low beneath the big window. Full height shelves lined the walls between the windows, of which there were several. Shelves that came about chest height ran through the room. About midway, a large arch opened into the rest of the room. The arches offered more shelf space and likely helped carry the load of a weight-bearing wall. This was no ordinary home library.

Desks were tucked in here and there, though Courtney knew the household's researcher, Riley always took the one furthest back. While Courtney couldn't see Riley, the creature inside Courtney could smell her. All of Courtney's senses had been getting stronger but it was the sense of smell that continued to surprise her. She could smell when someone was happy or sad and she knew where every single woman was in her cycle with just a sniff.

The cats, all of whom weren't quite ordinary cats, had their own musky scents and Courtney knew which was which by now.

Anastasia, the calico cat sitting beneath the tree, moved into a crouch, waiting.

Something was outside. Courtney felt it suddenly, the thing inside her recoiling. Normally it wanted to reach out and feed. While the rest of the household still called it a frost witch, Courtney thought of her creature as a vampire. She'd never felt it recoil from anything before.

She stood up, intending to go downstairs. The floors squeaked and groaned under Riley's ponderous walk as she hurried across the big room. Courtney waited, sensing, perhaps from the sounds, perhaps from the smells coming to her, that Riley wanted her to wait.

"Oh good, you're still here," Riley said.

Below, feet hurried to the door which squeaked gently as it opened.

"Why?" Courtney asked.

"It's the representative from Cat Home. Anastasia has word from Base Command that it would be best if you waited here." Riley watched her, perhaps hoping for some sign that Courtney understood.

Courtney hoped she gave nothing away. The creature inside her tried pushing at its cage, the bars of which Courtney had imagined into place, and Stuart, their Base Command representative, had helped solidify. It didn't like the Cat Home representative. If Courtney didn't know better, she'd have said the thing was afraid.

The feeling interested her. Until then, she wouldn't have said the frost witches had emotions. Normally they wanted to devour the energy of other people's emotions. Further, from everything Courtney knew, no one had encountered frost witches and survived so she didn't understand why the presence of any other creature would bother her frost witch.

Cat Home, of course, was the home world of the telepathic bond-mate cats, or so the stories went. The cats and those that created them dealt with the portals, something Courtney really didn't understand. She knew that most people didn't know about them and the creature inside her had come through one of them. She also knew that Cat Home had a different name but no one was able to pronounce it.

"Why?" Courtney asked Riley. The Cat Home representative clearly had nothing to fear from her or her passenger.

The frost witch waited, poised as if it were about to flee, though it had no place to go. The bars on the cage Courtney had created in her mind to keep the creature from possessing her held strong, at least for the moment.

"They need to get a feel for the house," Riley said. Her eyes went slightly unfocused. Courtney picked up a haze of static in her mind, the sense she had when the cats and their humans communicated telepathically.

"And they want to check out Chase first," Riley said. "Besides, with the snow today, no one is certain what will happen."

Courtney knew that. It's why she'd not been reading on her tablet, something she'd become accustomed to. She'd been restless all last night, the creature inside testing the cage walls, jumping at them. It had come to her then that it was going to snow and snow hard, soon.

She'd warned the others in the household, the clowder as they called themselves, and they'd closed the specially installed hurricane shutters. Matt had stayed on watch at the nearby portal, but Courtney knew, somehow, that the Cat Home representative had brought him back.

The temperature outside was dropping. Courtney felt it in her blood. She couldn't have described it better than that, only that she felt the coolness in the flow. The frost witches were on the ascendant.

Courtney wasn't sure if Cat Home had made the decision to send a representative here now because of the snow or if the snow was coming because of the representative. The two incidents were so intertwined that she didn't know how they'd unravel.

Sharp pain hit her beneath her ribs. Courtney drew in a breath. The pain felt icy cold. One of the bars of her prison had snapped. She closed her eyes, no longer worried about what Riley would pick up, and started focusing on rebuilding the bar. The frost witch hadn't done that before, hadn't been able to.

Whatever was going on had certainly given her creature a boost of power, something that hadn't happened in the month since Courtney had gained some control. On the edges of her consciousness, she heard Chase, her ex-boyfriend, who had his own frost witch, calling out, not just to her, but to someone else.

The witches had started causing trouble.

Before, they had started with mind games and manipulation. This time they were going directly for physical pain and, perhaps, injuries. Courtney wasn't sure if one was better than the other. Still, she was tired of the mind games, so she was thankful for that reprieve.

She stood up, still in pain but not nearly as much. Courtney had to get upstairs to her third floor room. She didn't feel ready to take on Chase or the representative from Cat Home, not when she was barely able to contain the thing inside her.

STUART

The clowder had begun to feel like home. Stuart had enjoyed a Thanksgiving meal, something Base Command never offered, and had even taken part in chats about gifts for Christmas. He'd helped decorate the two Christmas trees. One sat in the front room, in the window, looking festive. A tiny one sat upstairs in the library.

Several people had added lights to the outside and garland to the inside. He'd watched more holiday movies in the last month than he'd seen in a lifetime. A week ago, Stuart had begun to realize how much he enjoyed the camaraderie. He liked having people around he could chat with about inconsequential things.

The idea of going back to Base Command, working at his job, filled him with dread. Here, only Courtney, and sometimes Chase, could read his thoughts if he were careless. There, anyone could, really. He was the youngest of all of the Base Command representatives.

In his mind, Columbus, Ohio felt dark and claustrophobic. It might have been why he'd hated it when the hurricane shutters had been closed earlier in the day. He knew Courtney was right. Even he had felt the change in the air. This snow wouldn't be another little snow that dropped a few flurries and didn't stick. This was going to be big.

"Wilbur says that the representative from Cat Home is here," Trag said, telepathically. Stuart had become mind-bonded to the small black watcher cat a month ago. Trag's human, Chase, had told the cat to severe their connection as he felt something trying to escape through the link the month before. When the snows had begun in November, Trag had bonded with Stuart, both to boost their powers and to help Stuart remain in communication with the rest of the clowder.

The two weren't bond-mates exactly. Their bond was more superficial. Stuart did his best to keep the secrets of Base Command from Trag, though he knew he wasn't completely effective. Trag also kept secrets of his own, memories of better times with Chase that felt too personal to share. Stuart honored that in the same way Trag honored Stuart's secrets.

Stuart pushed himself away from the window where he'd watched the snow. His room was decent sized, certainly more than large enough for a real bed and dresser and desk. Instead, he had a mattress on the floor and an old dresser with a bottom drawer that squealed when you opened it. He preferred that, preferred that he had to wrap himself in an odd assortment of gifted linens and blankets. Not because he liked being gifted with things. He could have gone out and purchased those items easily enough. What he liked was not having belongings. It was discipline not to give in to certain desires. His original bond-mate Stardust had told him he would need to remain disciplined if he ever joined Base Command.

Stardust hadn't warned him how lonely he'd become as

his body changed into something not quite human. Stuart knew the cats forgot most of what they learned at Base Command, but as she was dying, Stardust had remembered some things. Stuart had only half heard her, not expecting that he'd be picked to join the workers at Base Command.

The room's carpeting was plush enough to squish beneath his feet, a luxury he didn't have a choice about. In the hall-way, he heard the rustle of movement from downstairs. The representative had just come through the portal. Chances were, Matt would bring the representative back to the clowder unless the representative felt it necessary for someone to remain on watch. However, given what was going on, Stuart had no doubt he'd find Matt had returned.

At the second floor landing, Stuart considered telling Courtney about the visitor. They had been long expected but the timing hadn't been known. Stuart felt the pull that was Courtney and her frost witch from the library. At the last minute, he decided against sharing with her. Stuart knew, somehow, that it wasn't his job to do so.

"What do you know about the representative?" Stuart asked. In his thoughts, he showed Trag some images so the cat would know he wanted as much information as possible, including a description.

"It has decided to come as a human," Trag said. *"Matt is uncertain if it is male or female. It is well-covered in clothing though Wilbur noticed that snow didn't touch it, falling around to the side as if it has a shield in place."*

"It probably does," Stuart said. The beings on Cat Home had bred the cats to monitor the portals. The portals allowed travel between worlds. All places, all worlds of any sort, existed within the realm of the portals. Like bubbles, the worlds floated, moving here and there, swirling around. Even in that chaos, there was a mathematical order and

Stuart understood the complex equations that would allow him to know which world was closest to theirs.

Cat Home had been waiting to send someone through the portal for weeks now. Apparently, this was the first time it was close enough for them to make it through in one jump. Jumping world to world could be wearing and they wanted their strength. It wasn't lost on Stuart that the frost witches had started the snow again on the same day.

He made it to the first floor. Kayley was in the front room. Short and compact, Kayley was the youngest of them. None of the cats had been on the first floor for the last week. Chase, again, causing problems.

The front room would have been a formal living room in an ordinary house. A nice sofa and a couple of wingback chairs faced each other for socializing. A coffee table sat in front of the sofa. A large wood-burning fireplace with beige and brown stone covered a third of the wall directly across from the entrance. A tall, decorated Christmas tree sat in front of the large front window. Gray shutters covered the glass so no one could see in or out.

Tenny and Tom were in the great room, which was directly behind the front room. Stuart could see them at the little nook area where they ate, the windows also covered in gray shutters. Last time, several of the windows had been smashed, but the clowder had managed to get them repaired right away. Stuart knew Base Command had been instrumental in making sure that happened. A bit of money and some persuasion by Darla went a long way.

The furnace clicked on. Stuart enjoyed the warmth blowing down on him. He stepped into the doorway by the great room to get closer to the warm air. He smelled the old coffee that always seemed to hover around this floor, making its way slowly up through the rest of the house at all hours of the day. If he was addicted to caffeine the smell would probably be strong enough to keep him awake.

Drew came out of his bedroom, looking worried. He seemed smaller, somehow, though he was still a big man. Stuart knew Drew hadn't lost weight since his ordeal but he wasn't quite himself. He tended to stay in his room, avoiding people if he could, which was not at all like the man Stuart had come to know in his first month.

Everyone appeared slightly tense, waiting. Of course, they'd have heard from their bond-mates what was happening. All except Drew. Stuart wondered what he knew. And how.

Moments later, the front porch creaked. Kayley got up and opened the front door, like a doorman. The day was as gray as the hurricane shutters covering the windows. Against that backdrop, Stuart noted Matt and Wilbur, first. Wilbur, the large, solid black cat hurried through the door, kicking a bit of snow from the bottoms of his feet.

There was already a good dusting of snow, perhaps a quarter of an inch, on the ground. Matt was closing an umbrella and throwing back the hood on his jacket. He had a hat on underneath. His hands were covered in thick black waterproof ski gloves.

Matt was average height and build, his hair a light brown. He wasn't as non-descript as Stuart, but if the ability to pass unnoticed played into getting asked to join Base Command, Stuart figured he'd see Matt there after Wilbur died.

Assuming they survived the frost witches.

The representative from Cat Home was also of average height. In fact, Stuart wondered if it had come through and mirrored Matt. The features on the face were more feminine but not so much that it looked womanly. Matt looked like a man. The representative was both and neither.

It looked around, brown eyes slightly larger than normal,

and took in the house, Kayley, Tenny, Tom, and finally Stuart. It continued to stare at Stuart as if waiting for something.

"*Ask...*" a whisper seemed to come into his mind. Not like Trag. Not even like Essalyn, the Base Command cat he'd been paired with for this job.

"What should we call you?" Stuart asked. He had no idea if that was what he needed to ask. Perhaps there was more. It would come.

"Call me Grey," it said.

"Then welcome, Grey," Stuart said. He didn't offer a hand. Had no desire to touch skin that he knew would be slightly chilled and just a wee bit slimy. He felt it all the time at Base Command to a lesser degree. He had no doubt this creature would feel the same way.

"Thank you," Grey inclined its head. Stuart knew there were ways of using gender-neutral pronouns for humans who didn't fall into the neat binary genders he'd come to think of as normal, but this creature wasn't human.

"So," Kayley said, "do you have a preferred pronoun?"

Grey looked perplexed. Stuart heard a faint buzz of telepathic communication in his mind. This was lower and faster than the sounds he caught when the cats spoke telepathically.

"I prefer 'he' or 'him,'" Grey said quietly after a moment.

Kayley nodded.

Matt finished taking off his outerwear and closed the door, but not before Stuart caught a glimpse of the snow falling hard enough to make it difficult to see the street beyond the lawn.

He caught the smell of something burning. Figured it was Grey's magic. He turned to see the representative from Cat Home watching him. Stuart could have sworn it looked different now but he couldn't quite figure out how.

CHASE

Chase was aware. That was about the best he could say. He certainly wasn't in control. The frost witch inside him had tricked him into giving up control.

If he had the ability to feel fear, he would be petrified but he was so distant from his body that such emotional reactions were beyond him. So he watched, dispassionate.

Deep down, Chase knew what was right and wrong. He knew the thing inside him wanted to devour everything and everyone. He felt it sucking energy from the ground around it and the people. The magical barrier that Stuart and Courtney had placed around it made it pause but didn't quite stop it. As it got hungrier and angrier, it tested the boundary, slithering around it to sneak quick sips of energy.

At some point, it would break through completely. Chase knew it held enough power in reserve to destroy the barrier.

Through the creature, Chase felt the thrum of life force being utilized by his body. He was linked to this thing for good or ill. It knew his thoughts before he did. Once, as he felt it draining the heat from the air and causing snow to fall, he'd tried to escape to the portal. Throwing himself through would have stopped it, but one of the clowder had stopped him.

Chase didn't even know who had stopped him, only that strong arms had prevented him from slipping out the back door and running through the snow. His decision had come last minute. The creature hadn't been ready to stop him, momentarily distracted by consuming the warm air. Now, it was too late. The frost witch watched him and his thoughts, always. In a way, it was pleased about the fact that he was locked in a cement room. It could continue to sip energy here and there, never quite enough to trip off the alarms set on the boundaries, but Chase was contained.

It didn't give Chase a chance to talk to anyone, to explain. He was allowed to be awake and aware when no one was around. The minute someone came, the frost witch took over.

Chase's entity hated the way Courtney treated hers. It couldn't quite get to her to siphon her energy and free the other frost witch. Somehow, she'd found a way to harness the entity's abilities for herself, though her frost witch continued to try and push its way out of the cage she'd created.

Though it wasn't at full power, Chase felt his creature reaching out and eating energy from the sky. He felt its disturbance. He didn't understand what was happening, but for the first time in a long time, Chase felt agitated, maybe fearful.

He didn't quite have control over his body, but he was closer to it than normal. The frost witch wanted him there, upfront. The image that came to mind was of a hostage situation, a gun to his head, his body used as a shield in a shootout. The creature was willing to let him die in whatever confrontation was coming.

Not that there was much he could do about it. Chase had

given up fighting for control. He couldn't win. He'd been waiting for death, though now and then he beat back the creature when it threatened the clowder, or when it threatened Trag.

Now that his death felt imminent, Chase realized he didn't really want to die. Unfortunately, he wasn't certain he had the power to stop the death he felt rushing towards him. He should have worked harder, found a way to work with Courtney more closely. There were things he knew she didn't understand yet, but he did. If he could let her know those things...

The creature cut off that train of thought before going back into hiding. Chase heard people moving about in the basement. Voices were just on the other side of the wall.

The frost witch wasn't testing the wall to see who it was. Chase's heart hammered. Maybe he could get real words out. Warn them about what needed to be done.

AMBER

Amber was in her office, across from the medic room, reading more information on acupuncture, when she heard people upstairs. Minnett was up on the second floor, watching out the library window with many of the other cats. Amber missed having the little tuxedo cat resting at her feet. Before the frost witches invaded the clowder, Minnett used to sleep in a bed beneath Amber's desk. Right next to Amber's feet. Amber had always appreciated the warmth and comfort of her bond-mate.

The plain desk held only her computer. The books shelved behind her were mostly upright, with only a few falling to the side. The light in the room was bright, and the air smelled vaguely of sweet smoke from moxa and that unique scent of books.

There wasn't much sound from above, simply because this part of the basement was well insulated. The medic room was designed to be quiet and much of the extra insulation had carried over to the little office assigned to the clowder's healer. The fact that she heard anyone meant there were many people moving around.

"The Cat Home representative is here," Minnett said. Amber was always aware of her cat, sharing her thoughts. She was vaguely aware that the snow was coming down harder than ever and the clouds lay so low over the land that they looked like fog. Minnett, however, had been watching for hours. Cats were far more patient than humans.

Amber thought it was interesting that the representative had arrived just after the snow had started again. *"What about Matt?"* Amber thought back.

"He's with him. Along with Wilbur. Wilbur says Matt isn't comfortable with the representative." Amber read Minnett's sense that there was no reason to be uncomfortable, a sort of equanimity that wasn't typical among humans who preferred things they understood.

Minnett's mind sent an image of a human-looking creature, which calmed Amber a bit as well. Given what the little cat had told her, she had worried about the representative looking odd. Instead, he or she looked terribly ordinary, though she didn't know if the creature was male or female or something else.

"Kayley has asked and it has chosen to be he and him," Minnett told her. *"He calls himself Grey."*

So it was a male who looked ordinary. She'd barely finished her conversation with Minnett when people began walking down the stairs. By the sounds of the thumping and squeaks, it had to be a large number of the clowder.

"Matt, Stuart, Tom, and Grey are all coming down," Minnett said. *"Kayley and Tenny are staying at their posts."*

Amber stood up. She was wearing her heavy black and white cat slippers along with black yoga pants and a red sweatshirt with the image of a black and white cat peeking out of the pocket. Her hair was pulled back. She needed a haircut but hadn't been out of the house very often in the last months. Her days and often her nights were spent reading and asking questions about possession on the internet.

By trade, Amber was an acupuncturist. While she and Minnett did a different type of healing, when she wasn't with the cat or was treating an ordinary problem, Amber used her needles. She'd made a dent in Courtney's possession using a treatment she had learned when researching. While she'd repeated the protocol, it hadn't appeared to make any further difference in Courtney. Still, Courtney was certain that it was that treatment that had allowed her to beat back the frost witch inside her.

So, for the last several weeks, Amber had spent time perusing acupuncture forums and searching acupuncture sites for more information on possession. She found the most esoteric treatments she could and read up on them. She'd ordered tomes of obscure information, even some in other languages when Minnett assured her that she could access someone at Base Command to allow her to translate the writing.

Those books that had yet to be read were piled on the floor. Another pile sat next to the bookshelf. Those were books Amber didn't plan to keep in her library because they hadn't offered her answers. Not that she expected to find such things, but she had to try. She'd been so obsessed with her search for information that she'd even missed decorating the house for Christmas.

She made it to the door about the time Stuart reached the big room at the bottom of the stairs. The main room contained a ruined pool table and a plain wooden subfloor, not yet covered in carpet. They'd been arguing about what color to get, as well as what to do with the pool table.

In beating back Chase and the frost witch inside him, Courtney had made it rain in the basement, destroying everything. Even the print of the cats playing poker had been ruined, though the stained glass cat lamp had survived. The tables and club chairs had already been removed and the room echoed a bit when you talked.

A single chair, newly purchased, sat in the hallway, also just a subfloor, though that part of the carpet had been minimally ruined. Amber had refused to allow them to pull up the carpet in her office. Fortunately, the medic room was all vinyl flooring and it had only been stained slightly from the puddles near the door.

Grey followed Stuart down to the basement. Amber understood what bothered Matt. Grey didn't seem to look the same from moment to moment. Almost like pictures flashing by rather than a steady face. It was disorienting.

"You would find his natural form worse," Minnett said. *"We cats know it, though Base Command had us forget. Once seeing him, seeing through the glamour, we know what they look like."*

"You are the healer?" Grey asked Amber. His voice was on the high end of normal for a man, but just a hair too low for a woman, unless she was a smoker.

"I am," Amber said. She felt like she ought to put out her hand to shake but she was reluctant to do so. She didn't want to touch Grey.

"He will feel slimy to you. It is what most humans say even about many who are at Base Command," Minnett explained.

Grey turned abruptly and nodded at the wall. "He's beyond there, isn't he?"

"Chase?" Amber asked. "He's down the hall slightly."

Grey gave her a long look. His eyes were brown, sort of, but their shade seemed to vary from moment to moment, but not from shadows falling across his face. This was like a bad movie, or someone intentionally trying to be crazy-making.

Minnett had no input on why his eyes changed colors slightly.

Grey turned and walked down the hallway. Anson had

been in a chair near Chase's door, but he was standing back, waiting. Amber noted Grey looking at the chair. He seemed to be examining it as if he'd never seen such a thing. Stuart held back. Matt and Tom waited with him, watching.

The door Grey stood in front of had been a hollow core interior door. Now they had a solid core door reinforced with plywood. A long metal bar was placed over it that could be raised and lowered when necessary. Four deadbolt locks evenly spaced kept the door locked. A new knob had been put on the now thicker door, the handle lock on the outside.

No one had bothered to paint the plywood so it was a typical golden brown. Grey examined it for some time, as if the idea of plywood was as new to him as the chair.

"It can get out whenever it wants. The door won't hold it." Grey said it as if they didn't know.

"So far he hasn't tried," Stuart said. Anson looked relieved that someone else was speaking. Amber noted Stuart's use of the pronoun "he" as if referring to Chase. Grey was clearly thinking only of the frost witch.

"No," Grey said, "it hasn't. It's been waiting, stealing energy. It's not gotten enough and that worries it. I feel humanity from it, so the clowder member remains in that body. To destroy the body will destroy him. He does not want to die."

Grey said all of that without inflection. He might have been a robot reading instructions, though his voice was more realistic than Siri or Alexa.

"Can we help him?" Amber asked.

Grey turned to look at her. She regretted speaking.

"We have found no way of saving anyone from the frost witches. How we know about them and why they disappeared for so long is only in the most ancient of our records. They say nothing about defeating the witches. Our researchers are continuing to investigate probabilities."

He sounded so cold and calculating. Amber felt Minnett agreeing with the description. She let Amber know that research included mathematical probabilities of what would work. A sense that sending Chase out through the portal, even killing his body would not stop the frost witch, just delay it. Cat Home worried the witches would find their world and destroy it. They wanted to stop the creature here, on Earth, not to save this world, but to keep theirs safe.

"We, too, want to live," Grey said. "Do not begrudge us that. If your lives seem less important to us, it is because they are so brief. Do you feel grief over every lost housefly?"

He didn't look at Amber this time. He was once again examining the lock. It was probably good because Amber felt her face heating at being compared to a housefly.

"It is not disrespectful. We hold all life in great esteem," Grey said. "This does not mean we understand it nor are we under the illusion that we can save everyone. Still, your world is a place where we can make a stand and perhaps save not only your world but other worlds. This is particularly true since you have at least one of your people who appears nearly in control of her frost witch. Even so, I feel the frost witch getting stronger and she is unlikely to maintain that control much longer."

Amber hated how Grey just seemed to know things he shouldn't.

"We are all telepathic," Grey said. "Else how would we create your bond-mates that look like your world cats but with full telepathic powers?" This time he turned. Amber didn't even see him move. He was just there, facing her instead of the lock.

Amber bit back a response. None was needed. If he wanted one, he knew she was trying not to embarrass herself by shuddering.

"I have examined your watcher. The creature cowers,

though it has pulled in as much energy as it can. The watcher is there, too, afraid. For the moment, I am potentially more powerful, though, alas, I do not know exactly which of my powers worries it most." Grey seemed perplexed. "The cats here, via those at your Base Command, have attempted low-level spells of the sort I can do but there appears to be no result. Not even a movement that might suggest more power would work. The human who controls her frost witch even adds her power to them sometimes and yet nothing happens. I do not understand what exactly it fears about me, yet I am certain it is purposely attempting to hide from me."

Grey seemed perplexed. What could Grey do that terrified the frost witch inside Chase? If the species on Cat Home had some power that terrified the frost witches, you'd think there would be a record of that.

Amber bit her lip and glanced at Stuart. He'd always seemed odd to her. She'd held him at arm's length. Yet here he was, clearly feeling the same things about Grey that she was. Maybe he was less alien than she thought.

COURTNEY

Courtney started pacing the floor up in her room while she waited. Her bedroom was tucked up on the third floor in a corner with a neat little daybed beneath a dormer style window. Turquoise and white pillows made the bed comfortable for sitting but Courtney was too agitated to be still.

The Cat Home representative had arrived. Feeling its telepathic exchanges, Courtney's senses told her the representative was both like and unlike the cats. In the same way, it was like and unlike the frost witches. In her gut, she thought that it was related to the frost witches, like maybe they were some rogue faction split off from the creatures at Cat Home.

Grey, that was the name the Cat Home representative wanted to go by, seemed to find that idea amusing but also interesting. Her frost witch disliked the idea, sending as much of a cold chill through Courtney as it could. That had always been the way the frost witch punished her. It made her cold, so cold she could hardly function. Now, locked in the psychic cage, it was limited. Still, Courtney felt the slight chill down her spine.

She tried to parse the emotions running through her, those that were hers and those that belonged to the frost witch inside her. Courtney wouldn't have said her frost witch was afraid exactly, that was her own emotion. Rather the frost witch was avoiding Gray. It would normally try and siphon energy from any emotion in the house, and there was plenty of it just then, but it didn't try to siphon from the Cat Home Representative. In fact, it avoided Grey like a child avoiding its medication.

By the time Grey and his entourage reached Courtney's room, she was tired of pacing. Her legs could have moved forever, but she was bored with the few steps she could take. She'd closed the door, though no one stood guard outside. She'd proven herself often enough. Stuart and Amber worked with her regularly and she kept them appraised of what she knew about the frost witch inside her.

It wasn't enough, of course. It never was.

When the door opened, Grey stood there, regarding her. Courtney didn't like it. She felt disoriented. The frost witch didn't like it for different reasons. Still, Courtney knew it was looking for weaknesses. Grey hadn't been on Earth very often. The mores of the people, the gravity, these things felt wrong to him. He wasn't quite balanced in the same way he was at his home.

Worlds changed those who lived on them. It wasn't exactly correct to say that people lived on worlds. Rather, they lived *with* worlds. There was a relationship between the world and the living being.

Anything coming through a portal would start to change in ways unique to each world. While Courtney had thought of watchers being placed to protect humans from alien creatures from other worlds, the watchers also protected those alien beings by sending them back as quickly as possible.

Most wouldn't notice the changes when they were sent back quickly. Even if they stayed in a world for a time, they might not understand what was going on, not like Grey did. He was prepared to have to go back through new changes upon returning to Cat Home. His understanding could be a weakness.

Grey said nothing for a long time, watching Courtney as she and the frost witch assessed him. He was making the same sorts of assessments. He didn't quite smell the way the other humans did. What he did have was a sort of blankness around scent. Perhaps part of the process of making himself look almost human.

"You are very astute for a person of your youth," Grey finally said. His voice was higher than Courtney would have expected. He held no accent to her ears but he spoke more formally than people typically did.

"Thanks?" Courtney said. Was it really a compliment?

"You have taken on the powers of the frost witch and you have imprisoned it with them. An interesting idea. It's working on taking back those powers but you have bought yourself and your world time." Grey stood there, not moving. Moving was hard for him. Courtney wasn't sure why. Another weakness. An easier one to exploit if his other powers weren't so great.

"You steal from the frost witch. It will turn on you when it can," Grey said. No inflection. He could be a robot.

Courtney knew that. The witch wanted out. It wanted to leave her and jump to someone else, someone easier to control, but she couldn't let it do that. Another person might not be able to fight.

"And you will die."

Her death had been looming before her for over a month

now. Courtney had asked for it on more than one occasion. She was prepared to be sent through the portal and die.

"Or the frost witch will find a way to siphon your life force without you being aware and then you will die," Grey told her.

An outcome Courtney hoped wouldn't happen. If it did, the creature would jump to another person.

"Your assessment of my powers is interesting. There were weaknesses I was not aware of. As I am aware of them now, I can take precautions," Grey said.

Courtney tried not to look so surprised that he had read what went through her mind and the mind of the frost witch so easily. The creature shrank back as if trying to hide from her as well. It didn't really fear Grey, but it didn't want him to understand it and perhaps learn how to destroy it.

"No. If we knew that, it would already be destroyed," Grey said.

Courtney was getting tired of the one-sided conversation. Stuart was watching from the doorway. She smelled the others behind him, Amber, Tom, and Matt, each with their own distinctive scent. Sometimes she heard their thoughts but she had to concentrate. It was easier when she let her entity feed off of them.

Stuart had told her to try, to see if that made it easier and it did. She often caught things from the telepathic communication with the cats. However, there was always so much communication going on that it was all white noise unless she tried to focus on one specific thread.

"Your garlic worked for you?" Grey asked.

Courtney had thought to use garlic because vampires didn't like it. It had helped her remain in control. She wasn't wearing a string of garlic but she always carried a few bulbs around with her. When she felt as if the frost witch was getting stronger, she'd often smell the bulbs to put herself back in control. She kept the creature just fed enough so that it remained somewhat complacent. Sometimes she'd notice it gaining in power and she'd return some of that energy to the ground.

"Yes," Courtney said. She wanted to snap that he knew it did but didn't want to get on Grey's bad side.

"We have records of your vampire legends. The areas that we believe the frost witches appeared before were nowhere near this world. We find it unlikely that they were the basis for your legends."

Courtney shrugged. Maybe the monsters were related the way she was certain Grey was related to them. She felt his discomfort with the idea. The frost witch did, too. It would use that if it could, though it hadn't figured out how yet.

"So what next?" Courtney asked.

"I have examined the two of you. I must report in. Is there a room?" Grey asked, turning to Stuart.

"There are a couple down the hall," Tom said, acting as host.

Courtney watched Grey go. Her body eased, more relaxed the moment he was out of sight, but like a person in pain waiting for the ache to return, she wasn't quite as relaxed as she might be if he were completely gone. He was unsettling. His abilities dwarfed hers, though she felt that she was the more powerful.

Her frost witch was eager to be let out to fight. Courtney slapped it back, redoing the bars of the cage. She'd been working on that weaving since it had broken one. She couldn't let it run free, not then.

An idea was working its way through her subconscious. She felt it in the feelings and impressions she had. Maybe it belonged to the frost witch. Maybe not. Whoever it belonged to, Courtney was certain the idea was important.

DREW

Sudden fatigue overcame Drew more quickly than any illness he'd ever had. He'd gotten some stomach bug once. One moment he'd felt fine, perhaps a little chilly, but other than that, he'd have said normal. He'd bent down and put laundry in the dryer and by the time he stood up, it was all he could do to get himself back to his apartment and into bed. This fatigue had come on faster.

He'd been reading in the big chair in his room. He felt better in the room rather than out in the great room where he'd normally have read. He liked the sofa, the way the cushions cuddled him, and the warmth. Usually, there was a fire going and people around to distract him and talk to him so he didn't get lonely. Now, since he'd died—and wasn't that something he'd never expected to say?—he preferred his room.

Courtney had used the frost witch's powers to bring him back. He'd been dead for almost 24 hours, frozen, again by Courtney, to preserve his body. She'd pulled him back. Drew had no memory of that pulling. Since then, the clowder, even his bond-mate, who was no longer his bond-mate, the tele-pathic link severed by death, didn't trust him.

Mack, the big orange tabby who had been so well matched with Drew, both easy-going, big guys, something that had felt like a joke to Drew, spent most of his time in the library, now. Most of the cats did because they didn't trust Chase. Mack did because he didn't trust Drew. He didn't even twine around his legs when Drew took food up to him.

The distrust hurt.

Drew had taken to hiding in his room. He appreciated the big recliner he had in there where he could read. Mack used to sleep on it regularly. Drew hoped that one day the cat would come back and snooze there, even if he wasn't ready to re-forge their bond.

Light fell across the room from outside, but not so bright that Drew hadn't needed a lamp. He preferred a lamp to the overheads. The day was gray and he wasn't surprised when the snow began falling. He'd spent a little time staring at it, watching as the flakes began to stick to the narrow ledge outside his window.

His room might be on the first floor, but the deck outside didn't go all the way across. His window didn't get shuttered when Courtney and Stuart announced the snow was coming and they should close up the house. Drew felt both lucky and dismissed by that.

So he'd continued to read, trying to keep his mind on the latest Beeks novel by Michael W. Lucas. Lucas was self-published which always made Drew suspicious—if you were good, shouldn't an editor want your stories?—but Lucas had pulled him in and his quirky characters wouldn't let him go. Drew would have given anything to have Beeks' abilities.

She was confident where he was hesitant. She didn't care if people didn't like her. Drew worried about that all the time. He hated not being trusted, but he couldn't even trust himself.

He'd barely finished the chapter when his head began to nod. It wasn't boredom. He could hardly wait to find out what happened next. He struggled to keep his eyes open so he could read further but ultimately he had to lie down.

Drew was asleep even before he finished crawling into bed, his body moving from muscle memory to find a place where he'd be comfortable enough to stay asleep.

"About time," Chase said.

"What?" Drew asked. He knew he was dreaming. He remembered going to his bed.

For the moment he seemed to be in the basement room with Chase. Drew knew that this wasn't exactly a dream, even if his body was asleep upstairs.

Around him, in Chase's makeshift cell, the floor and walls were all concrete. The ceiling had been finished off, covering over the electrical and plumbing and heating and cooling pipes. The concrete made it stay cool. Chase had an old futon someone had dragged down to sleep on. Someone else had brought him a small two-foot by three-foot rug for his feet.

They'd had someone install a bathroom in there, a small shower, toilet, and sink. It was barely big enough to go in and turn around in. After, Anson had welded a ring in the center of the room, and Chase was bound by a chain.

Drew thought it was barbaric. When Chase came to him in dreams, he never seemed bothered by it, but Drew was. He wondered if he'd be the next one to be chained in a room so he couldn't leave.

"Grey is here," Chase said.

Drew thought he'd heard the door open just as he'd been heading to the bed. Couldn't quite remember, though.

"Who is that?"

"Cat Home," Chase told him. "He's not human. You'll need to take care of him. He'll see it coming from me."

"I don't understand," Drew said. Deep down, he knew Chase was asking him to kill the Cat Home representative. He didn't want to. Chase often gave him things to do that he didn't want to do. Mostly he avoided them. Sometimes, though, the suggestion was so great that he wasn't able to stop.

He'd been working with Stuart to gain control. No one had been able to keep Chase from sneaking into his dreams that weren't exactly dreams. Stuart and Courtney both had put spells around him to try and keep Chase out, or at least warn them when he got in, but no matter what, Chase was able to circumvent their little protections.

"You understand perfectly," Chase said. "You don't want me to die, do you? That creature will kill me."

Drew wasn't sure what creature Chase was talking about. Was he calling the representative a creature or was he talking about the frost witch inside him? If Drew interpreted it as the latter, perhaps he could deal with whatever Chase was asking.

"Kill it!" Chase said.

"How?" Drew asked.

"Sneak attack. It's too powerful otherwise. No one thinks you have any power, but you've been lightly infected. You can do it. You have more magic than you think. And you're strong," Chase said.

He didn't sound like the Chase Drew knew. This man was practically frothing at the mouth. Drew hated these dreams. He hated being told to harm someone. Chase had even asked him to kill Trag, coaching it as a "put him out of his misery because we're not bonded anymore." Drew had avoided hurting Trag, though the cat never spent time alone with him.

It hurt to be so distrusted even if he understood. It frustrated him that they seemed more trusting of Courtney who was possessed by her own creature when he'd only been lightly infected by Chase's. It wasn't fair.

"It's not. And Cat Home is making it worse," Chase said. "But don't think about what you're going to do. He's psychic. Really psychic. Just do it. It's your only chance. He'll kill you if you fail."

And like that Drew was awake. He looked longingly at the Kindle on the little chest near the chair. He wanted to go back and hide in that story, not his own.

STUART

Stuart didn't like the energy between Courtney and Grey. He felt as if he were watching two fighters sizing each other up, waiting for a confrontation. He wasn't sure who he would bet on. Grey had experience and ability. Courtney, though… the frost witch gave her raw power the likes of which Stuart hadn't seen before.

Grey left with Tom, leaving Stuart and Amber behind. Stuart didn't want to talk there. Grey would know what was said, every bit of it. Stuart wasn't at all certain he wanted Courtney to know. She sank down onto the daybed.

"He frightens the creature," she said. "He was right, though, that the frost witch was making note of every weakness she could see through my eyes. Her advantage is that she has me. I know what human limitations are. I've felt them. Grey knows them in theory but hasn't lived them. He never will."

"What do you mean?" Amber asked.

"I got the sense that being here on Earth changes him sort of. He's not been here before or if he has, it's been so long that it doesn't matter. Are they immortal?" Courtney's abrupt change of topic surprised Stuart. She was looking at him, clearly hoping he could answer.

"Not exactly," Stuart said softly. So far as he knew the beings who lived on Cat Home eventually died, though their lifespan was closer to geologic age than human. "They are very long-lived, though."

"How long?" Amber asked.

"Eons in Earth years," Stuart said. "They probably remember this world when dinosaurs walked. They'd even have had something guarding portals then, too."

"They don't always use cats?" Amber sounded surprised. Stuart supposed that was to be expected. He'd never talked about what he knew. He wasn't normally supposed to.

"*You may explain.*" The voice wasn't familiar to Stuart, but he knew it was Grey.

"They create a physical body for whatever they need to guard the portals, preferably one that won't stand out. Here, for the last several centuries they've used cats. I think at one time it was a bobcat rather than a domestic cat," Stuart said. "Cats work for them because they're good at hiding and they're also small predators. They know how to protect themselves and to hunt naturally so Grey's people don't have to try and create those instincts."

Amber nodded. "So they just make them magic and telepathic?"

"*They won't understand,*" Trag said.

He was right. They wouldn't understand that the cats had been bred from beings on Cat Home who took the feline form and came to Earth, sacrificing themselves to breed in their abilities. Now and then one of the older beings would come here and live out the end of their life in a cat body so the powers wouldn't get diluted.

"They came here, originally, as cats," Stuart said, "and

bred the lines." He'd leave out the part about them coming back sometimes.

"What are they?" Amber asked.

"Shapeshifters," Stuart said. She had to know that. Minnett would know that by now. The cats were recovering the memories Base Command would have wiped from them thanks to the representative.

"And they shifted to cats, bred here, and went home?" Amber asked.

"The earliest of them went home again. Most stayed," Stuart said. All of it was involved in portal history, ancient portal history. Like the frost witches, the origins of the portals was almost legendary.

Amber turned and left.

Stuart nodded at Courtney.

"You're becoming like him, aren't you?" Courtney said. Stuart knew she was talking about Grey.

"I changed when I went to Cat Home, yes," Stuart said. He didn't want to answer her question but it seemed like she, or the frost witch inside her, understood more than made him comfortable.

"But you're still changing. It wasn't just that their world reset your body, in that relationship with worlds, it changed something fundamental so you're becoming like they would be if they lived here. It didn't stop. Does it stop for him when he comes here and goes back?" Courtney asked.

"Their bodies were made to change," Stuart said. "Our cells are less adaptable. Once they're set to change into something, they don't like to go back."

Courtney nodded. "It's why the cats stay here and don't go back to Cat Home."

"They can go back if they like. Sometimes those that lose a human go there," Stuart said.

Trag hadn't asked. Mack hadn't either, so far as Stuart

knew, but both cats were waiting, hoping to get their humans back. If one were to go, Stuart expected it would be Trag. Mack was older and set in his place here in the clowder.

Courtney looked thoughtful. She appeared to be thinking. Stuart looked behind him. The door was open but no one else was there. "I should go," he said quietly.

She gave him a half a nod and then went back to thinking.

"She's put up a barrier around the house," Trag said. *"There are people on the street looking at the house. Several have tools. One has a rifle."*

Each time the people around them got more violent about coming inside. *"Has Riley heard anything about accidents or murders?"* Stuart asked. Not that he could do anything about them from there, but that was another thing that seemed to ramp up with the snow.

"Nothing yet," Trag said. Yet, of course, the keyword.

Stuart walked down the hall to his room. Tom was coming out of a room on the end, where he'd gotten Grey settled. Stuart knew it held a king-sized bed with a plush mattress. The closet was the size of a bathroom and the bathroom itself was pretty spectacular if you went in for that sort of thing. He'd turned it down before walking all the way through the door.

He was curious about Grey checking in. He had questions but he'd learned that Base Command and Cat Home decided when you needed to know something, not him.

"Several of the people have fallen to the ground outside. I did not see them move. Nor did I sense any magic from Courtney," Trag said.

From down the hall, Stuart smelled something burnt, like a candle just snuffed out. It was the scent he caught whenever cat magic was being used. It had to come from Grey.

He hurried down the hallway. "What have you done to

the neighbors?" The clowder had always operated under the rules that no one should know who or what they were.

"I suggested they were all too tired to wait around outside the house, potentially testing that nice shield your girl has put up. Fine work for an amateur," Grey said. "Powerful enough that I'm not sure I'd get through it. But we don't need an audience."

"The people never remember. When the temperature drops too low, they'll freeze," Stuart said.

"Then let's hope the chill wakes them," Grey said. "They are not my concern right now. If I take the time to focus on saving them, I'll lose time studying the frost witches. If I am not able to find a weakness, the humans will die anyway."

"You took the time to knock them out," Stuart said.

"Because their thoughts were irritating," Grey snapped. "As are yours."

The look he gave Stuart sent Stuart backing out of the room as fast as he could. He didn't slam the door but closed it softly using every technique and trick he could to try and keep his thoughts to himself. Even so, it didn't feel like enough.

AMBER

Amber sat on the great room sofa. Tenny was curled in the corner of it. Tom was over on the maroon chair that sat nearby. Minnett was upstairs with the cats in the library, both to avoid Chase and because they could watch the outside world from up there. Stuart sat on the raised hearth made of brown stone, the gas fire dancing behind him. Kayley leaned against the doorframe so she could technically be at her post in the front room. It didn't matter that much, really.

Everything was closed up and locked down. Courtney had set up a shield around the exterior of the house against the incursions of the neighbors.

Tenny had a rich mocha coffee from their machine. Amber noted the way Tenny wrapped both hands around the cup as if she were trying to warm them as much as drink the splendid smelling brew.

The room wasn't cold, but Amber understood the desire. Deep down she felt as if cold was coming. Certainly, when she'd checked the weather on her phone the temperature was once again in free-fall. This morning it had been in the low forties. In only a few hours it was down to the low twenties and continuing to fall. Last storm, the low had hit seven below. Duluth had had a warmer day than Lexington.

"We need to keep our thoughts to ourselves as much as possible," Stuart said. "It's not that we need to be secretive, but because Grey finds too much telepathic noise distracting."

Amber wasn't sure to how to keep her thoughts to herself.

"*I can block you a little,*" Minnett said. "*In fact, all the cats have done so.*"

"So the cats have us blocked. What else?" Tenny asked.

Stuart didn't move. His stillness reminded Amber of Grey's stillness, though Stuart had a few ticks. In the months that he'd been at the clowder house, he'd begun to act more human than when he'd first arrived. Now, he was reverting to the man who had turned up on their doorstep during the first snow.

"Grey is checking in. If we're lucky, when he reached out to silence the people outside he found something that can be useful to us. I know that he and Courtney appeared to be sparring, but he was learning about the creature inside her," Stuart said.

With any luck, Grey would come back with a plan. Amber wasn't sure she trusted luck. It hadn't been with them so far.

"*The people outside have managed to drag all their downed friends inside various homes,*" Minnett replied. "*I have just watched a man sling a woman over his shoulder and walk off.*"

The actions out there made Amber wonder if whatever Grey had done had cut the neighbors off from the influence of the frost witches or if the witches needed people alive.

"*Riley says that the news includes four stabbings, two gunshot wounds, and thirty-five assaults with no weapons since this morning. There have also been more than the usual amounts of car accidents,*" Minnett reported. "*I do not believe those people were just*" *being nice to their neighbors. I believe the frost witch influenced them to take those people inside simply because dying in the snow did not generate enough emotion.*"

At the end of the commentary, Amber had pictures of torture from Minnett and she shuddered. They couldn't go out and rescue everyone from the influence, at least she didn't think so.

"*It is sort of our job,*" Minnett pressed.

"I don't believe it's our job today," Stuart said, partly covering his face with his steepled fingers. "I believe our job is to find the root of this. To go out trying to trim those branches would prevent us from doing that, though I have hopes with Grey here that he can read a bit of what's going on in the minds of those who have been influenced."

"We do more waiting while he figures out what we ought to do." Tenny pushed her body back against the sofa like she was fighting it. Her head lay back on top of the cushions. Her scalp was covered with thick tight curls.

Normally Tenny's hair was cut so short that Amber could see traces of her skin beneath the curls. It had grown out a bit. Everyone had other things on their mind. Besides, fighting the frost witches with slightly longer hair wouldn't matter. It's not like the witches did much physical fighting. It was all magic and psychic manipulation. Too bad they didn't have a trained therapist in the group.

"Are there any therapists in the clowders?" Amber asked.

"Why?" Stuart looked interested.

"We keep fighting this thing that's manipulating us. Maybe a therapist could give us tips on how to fight." Amber shrugged. "Or how to heal."

Stuart said nothing. Amber wasn't sure if he took her ideas seriously.

The door down the hall creaked open. Heavy footsteps approached. Amber watched, wondering what Drew wanted.

Though he had shadows in his energetic body, he had yet to have anything that looked as if it stuck. Each possession or influence was unique. Amber had yet to get a handle on what was going on with Drew. He was both with them and secretive. She knew he reported things Chase told him to Stuart yet she always had this sense that he was hiding other things.

"Chase wants me to kill Grey," Drew said. "Soon." He doubled over as if in pain. Amber stood up to hurry to him.

Before she was halfway across the room, she was spun back against the sofa, the air knocked out of her lungs.

"What the…" Tenny trailed off. She wasn't looking at Drew. That much Amber knew. Unfortunately, her body ached too much to turn her head towards the side where Tenny was looking.

"Grey has stopped you from going to Drew," Minnett said. *"He sees something. Something even I haven't been able to see, nor Stuart."*

Suddenly protective Drew, who just moments ago had been her greatest annoyance, Amber pushed herself up. She fought for a breath and then glared over at Grey who had moved silently down the stairs and into the great room.

"He was just reporting what someone told him," Amber snarled, fists clenched. She was ready to take on the representative from Cat Home herself if she needed to. She might not be able to heal him, but Drew was her patient. She wasn't about to see him harmed.

"He wasn't talking to Chase. The frost witch has a link to him. As it gets stronger it can leap from Chase into him or into anyone near him," Grey said.

Drew's eyes widened and he shuffled back out of the great room.

Amber watched him go, not surprised that his first thought would be to get away from people he might harm.

Courtney often wondered if her powers changed or if she just learned new things. She knew, for instance, when Grey laid a spell on the people outside her little shield to make them fall asleep. She felt their life force drop as many of them fell so deeply asleep that it might be better termed a coma. Having never been a nurse, Courtney didn't know why she knew that they were closer to being comatose than sleeping but she did.

The frost witch inside her was so active trying to get out, Courtney held her bulb of garlic to her nose, sniffing it. She tasted the spice in the back of her throat so strongly it made her want to gag. It was only minimally effective in slowing down the witch.

Amber had encouraged Courtney to try colloidal silver earlier in the month, but it hadn't done much for her. Perhaps it was about belief and she didn't actually believe that colloidal silver would work the way regular silver worked against vampires. She knew, on some level, it was silver, but that didn't seem to matter.

Courtney let her hand fall to the bed, still holding the

bulb. She was on the white and teal daybed. She'd made up the covers so they were neatly done. The blinds were open letting in gray daylight. She loved and hated the days when the sun was shining, the light hitting the floor in a golden puddle in her room.

The Courtney part of her wanted to lie down on the carpet and bask in that sunshine. The frost witch inside wanted nothing to do with the light. You'd think it could eat the energy. She'd actually let the witch do that, pulling the life force from the sun but the sunshine didn't change. Perhaps the frost witch was terrified of the sun because it couldn't overpower it.

While legends said the witches ate the suns of the worlds they took over, Courtney wondered. It was possible, but there would need to be a lot of frost witches to do that and she wasn't convinced there were that many of them. Legends could be wrong. Riley had suggested that one of the worlds the witches destroyed might have been nearing death anyway and the sun became a black hole and the legends were born.

Courtney didn't care. She just knew that her witch didn't like sunshine and didn't seem to be able to overpower the warmth from the light. So whenever there was sunshine, Courtney often laid in it just to annoy the creature.

It would retaliate by taking as much energy from her body as it could. Courtney would feel chilled but not freezing. She had the frost witch well in hand.

Sitting on the bed, with her bulb of garlic, Courtney tried something she'd never tried before. It hadn't been necessary, before. She hadn't trusted the frost witch to be truthful. It probably wouldn't be now, but perhaps she could gain a clue.

Courtney crossed her legs like she saw people do in yoga classes, straightened her back, and closed her eyes. Her right hand held the bulb of garlic. She breathed in and out, the way

Stuart had taught her. He hadn't insisted she sit in any particular way, but Courtney liked this way. It made her feel like a real meditator.

She focused on following her breath down, getting comfortable. Settled, she pictured the cage with the frost witch. She'd not done that unless her consciousness was on high alert. In this meditative, semi-conscious state, she was a little worried about purposely visiting the thing. Courtney wasn't sure what would happen.

The bars she'd created held. The broken one was repaired. She noted the long twining ropes of garlic that held the creature away from the bars. In her mind's eye, the cage hung suspended from a dark ceiling so high she couldn't see it. Everything around the cage was dark and, other than the chain it was suspended from, it touched nothing.

"What?" the frost witch asked. The vague white fog that had been inside the cage became a woman shaped figure, all in pale white like an ice sculpture that moved.

"Why does Grey bother you?" Courtney asked. She didn't picture herself in that place. She just pictured the frost witch.

"What will you give me if I tell you?" the witch asked. She was less ice sculpture and more flash-frozen body now.

"A few sips of life force," Courtney said.

"Can I take a cat?" the witch asked. She was fully female now. Prettier than Courtney in every way. Her body was lightly curvy and her face perfect with its short, slightly upturned nose and full lips. Her eyes were large and wide and the blue of the Caribbean Sea.

"No," Courtney snapped. "You won't kill anyone."

The witch thought about it. Courtney breathed in and out, feeling the weight of the garlic in her hand.

"Grey is like me, but he controls it well," the witch said.

"What do you mean like you? Magic?" Courtney asked.

"Magic, yes. Shapeshifter yes. He is my kind but not my

kind. Left long ago because he wanted to keep pets." The witch spit the last word like it was a bad thing.

"The cats?" Courtney asked, not certain what the witch meant.

"The cats are part of them, the ones like Grey, left behind on planets. They come in all shapes and sizes—some that would terrify you, others that would endear themselves to you more than those cats, which I know you hate."

The witch was wrong about hating cats. Courtney might not be completely easy with them, but she wasn't afraid of them any longer—and not just because she had the power to protect herself.

"Grey wants power, but he wants power over life forms. I live to devour, which is where he began. He is an old one, though I don't remember him personally. We breed differently than you, and I was gone before Grey was formed," the witch said.

"You mean you're from Cat Home?" Courtney asked.

"We are from the world that went on to colonize the world you call Cat Home," the witch corrected. "In the ages I have existed, I have seen many worlds come and go. Some are gone because of me and my kind. Some created monsters to oust us. Other worlds are gone simply because it was their time."

"What is your kind?" Courtney asked. She filed away the creation of monsters. Something to ask Riley to look into. Or maybe Grey, though she didn't want to talk to him, not really.

"I am like Grey. I am his kind. Ask him how he will die when the time comes," the witch said.

Courtney didn't like the smile.

"I expect my sips of life force," the witch snapped.

Courtney fled the place in her mind where the cage hung in the dark. She opened her eyes, half afraid that she'd find herself in the field of dying flowers. She heard the witch chuckle at her.

No field waited for her. She was in her room, her legs crossed over each other, her back straight, a teal and white pillow pressing lightly against her back.

Courtney straightened, wondering what Grey would say when she asked him what the frost witch had meant by her question. She felt a chill go down her back. Felt the frost witch demanding her payment.

Reaching out, Courtney found the people down the road up and about in their house. She let the witch take a few sips, more than she probably should have, but not so much that the witch harmed anyone, nor did the witch gain enough power to escape the cage Courtney had built.

It would do for now. She slipped off the bed and went in search of Grey.

STUART

Stuart tried to keep his expression neutral as he watched Amber catch her breath. His muscles were tensed, ready to help her stand back up. He didn't need to let Grey know how angry he was, no more than he already had.

"I am blocking you as much as possible," Trag said. *"Although I am not at all certain he cares what you feel. Feelings don't seem to mean anything to him."*

Stuart found the thought interesting. He didn't remember struggling quite this much on his visit to Cat Home. That had been years ago and there hadn't been a threat like this facing them. He also hadn't met anyone who felt as powerful as Grey. In the same way Base Command allowed visitors to only see those who looked most human, apparently Cat Home had allowed those visiting from Base Command to only see those who worked well with humans. Grey clearly wasn't one of those.

Amber adjusted her position on the sofa a bit. She glanced over at Tenny who was poised to attack, though Stuart knew that was futile.

He raised a single hand. Tenny backed down, though she glared at him. It said something about their level of trust in him that they listened. Stuart would laugh if he could because this was the one time they absolutely shouldn't trust him. He wasn't in control of anything.

"We can't be expected to know all that. Sometimes a verbal command is useful with humans," Stuart said. He kept his inflection neutral in the same way he might have reported something to one of his supervisors at Base Command.

"I forget you use your voices and not your thoughts," Grey said. He didn't appear sorry. Stuart didn't expect that.

"Has Cat Home found any clues in the things you've observed?" Stuart asked. Grey wouldn't necessarily observe just with his eyes and ears, the way humans tended to think of observation. He'd look on the energetic levels. Grey would see far more on those levels than Stuart could. Grey would also make connections that humans might not make simply because he thought so differently.

"Not so far," Grey said. "We are uncomfortable with the energetic signatures, though. They are similar to the signatures of our own magic."

"Does that mean your magic can counter theirs?" Amber asked, leaning forward.

Stuart wouldn't have considered that, not quite so quickly. But if the magics had similar signatures, they should interact more completely.

"My magic already has," Grey said. "As has the magic of your cats. It can slow them down, can do shielding spells. Stuart has worked with the one human who has joined with the frost witch to create more spells to bind the frost witches in the house."

"I don't think Courtney would say she's joined," Amber said.

Stuart waited for Grey to explain. It was an interesting choice of words. While Grey didn't understand humans very much, language was important to those at Cat Home. When they spoke, they tended to be precise. Their telepathic communications could sometimes be scattered and frustrating, but their words…those tended to be precise.

"Whatever she says, she is joined. There is no getting the witch out of her. I can't begin to see where her energy begins and the witch's ends. When we have taken care of any other witches here, she will need to be killed," Grey said.

Stuart felt a sharp pain in his gut. Regret and sorrow. He'd become fond of Courtney. He didn't always understand how she saw the world, but she'd worked hard to contain the witch. The idea of killing her… he hoped he wouldn't be the one tasked with doing it, though he had no desire to ask any of the others to do so.

"And Chase?" Amber asked.

"He has not joined. The frost witch appears to have taken over his body but his spirit is hidden, keeping himself apart. To gather the power to protect herself, Courtney allowed her consciousness to join with the witch. Now it is a matter of will. For now, the girl is winning but the witch has the power and ages of experience. It is waiting and leaning." Grey crossed his arms.

Stuart listened to someone coming down the stairs. Light steps. Courtney. She rarely came down to the first floor. She'd been the first to suggest she remain upstairs, further from Chase, yet here she was.

Courtney paused behind Grey. Her head came up to Grey's shoulders. She was dressed in flannel pants and a purple long-sleeved t-shirt. Her feet had on heavy purple socks that matched the t-shirt, although the cream and pink flannel pants weren't quite in the right shade.

"What happens to you when you die?" Courtney asked. She was looking at Grey.

Stuart didn't know what her question meant. Grey's facial expression didn't change but there was a pause, an energetic pulling back that suggested he was surprised by the question.

"It's not important," Grey said.

"I think it is," Courtney said.

"You or the witch you carry?" Grey kept his arms crossed. He gave Courtney a hard look. Something in the way his eyes fastened on her, let Stuart know Grey was looking at her energetic body.

"The witch told me to ask you. It seemed like a good question," Courtney replied. Her right hand was in the pocket of her flannel pants, probably gripping her garlic bulb. She'd taken to doing that when she was nervous, as if her nervousness and anxiety might let the frost witch out. Given the way the witches worked, it just might.

"When we become too mentally infirm that we are a danger to others, our bodies are sent into the planet's sun," Grey said.

"But aren't you dead first?" Courtney asked after she winced a bit.

"As shapeshifters, our cells are constantly renewing. On rare occasions, there are missteps such that one may not survive. As we age, our telepathic powers start to fade and we often go into dementia. It is then we are sent out to the sun." Grey seemed to have no worries about that.

"Are you sure that those sent to the sun actually die?" Courtney asked.

It dawned on Stuart that the frost witch could be suggesting that it was the same species as the Cat Home natives. That would make it related to the cats. A creature as powerful as Grey with dementia? That seemed too horrible to contemplate. And if there were many, for there must be, given the age of the Cat Home species, what chance would any world stand against the chaos?

"I shall check in with the elders at Cat Home," Grey said stiffly. He turned and walked out of the room.

Courtney stood looking back at him.

Stuart put his hands down and thought about it. What did it mean if frost witches who sucked the life force from a planet started from the same magical place that the cats did? And what did that mean for those like him who started as one thing but traveled to Cat Home and were forever changed?

"I feel a truth in the thought," Trag said slowly. *"It would be why it knew we were the danger, too."*

"If they come from Cat Home what do we do?" The implication of a being with that much power not being fully able to control itself terrified Stuart.

He dropped his head into his hands, waiting for an answer from Trag that never came. The cat clearly had no answer to a question that was only half rhetorical.

CHASE

wake and aware, Chase sat on the edge of the bed in the basement. A chill surrounded him. For once he didn't believe it was due to the frost witch. The chill remained because this room had never been meant for human habitation. It was a storage and mechanical room repurposed as a room to hold him, or rather, the frost witch.

The frost witch, of course, could have left any time. For now, it was learning.

Chase hated feeding it information. He did his best to stay apart from the creature, creating his own little cage, a mental space into which the frost witch wasn't allowed. There, Chase made up lies about the way the world worked, hoping to confuse the creature. It was all he could do.

Upstairs, people walked around. The frost witch inside him longed to drink their life force. Chase felt it shimmying its way through the shields around the room to take a quick sip here and there. It couldn't go too far out nor could it stay long but it had figured out how to take quick sips of energy, enough to keep it alive.

Greedy for more life force, it always wanted more. Now

that greed had turned into need. It thought it needed more to take on Grey.

Images of another sort of life reached Chase. He knew suddenly that even if he leaped through a portal into a dead zone, it wouldn't kill the frost witch inside. The witch would become dormant and would seek out a living creature should a ship pass through or should life be found on a newly seeded world.

Chase chewed on the term "seeded." The idea of seeding worlds, as if life was planned, rocked him. While he wouldn't say that he was particularly religious, he'd grown up in a household where such beliefs were taken seriously. The idea of aliens had shaken him at first. The idea that aliens were seeding worlds and were, perhaps, a source of life made him reel.

He wanted to reject the idea, but it stuck with him, the creature feeding off his distress and confusion. Chase cut it off as quickly as he could. Now he wasn't just cool, he was cold.

He really had nothing to do all day but think. He'd been thinking and wondering for hours a day. As soon as someone came to the room, Chase was locked back in his cage as the creature took over, teasing and threatening the rest of the clowder.

As soon as they were gone and the creature became bored with its prison, Chase was released. Solitary by nature, Chase didn't mind being alone. He minded not being out in the world. He pictured the park with the trees, the sounds of birds singing their songs, the chipmunk and squirrel feet crunching lightly against fallen leaves.

He tried to remember the damp smell of the earth and the fallen leaves, the scent of sap that might come from a tree, the faint traces of exhaust that would float through the park from the street. He missed that. Missed sitting with Trag, who smelled of cat and talked to him through their telepathic bond.

Chase tried to build this image as a house around himself in the dark and dank cellar that was his prison.

"*So you are there,*" a voice said. Telepathic. Not the creature, though Chase thought it felt similar.

Chase's thoughts were cut off. In his mind, he saw a hand slapping his mouth before he could utter a sound.

A door slammed against the voice. The frost witch who looked like Courtney but more perfect leaned back against the literal image of a door. The thoughts and dream spaces it often forced Chase into played into subconscious puns from time to time.

The witch wore pink and white, the blonde hair a bit lighter than Courtney's, the features a bit more even. It looked as fragile as Courtney did sometimes.

"What?" Chase thought, staying on his side of his mind. He practically drew a line between them.

"It stays out," Not-Courtney said.

"I don't have the power to keep something out," Chase said quietly.

"I do." The witch walked over to him. "Are you sure you don't want to join me?"

The pink and white clothing dropped away. Chase tried to close his eyes or turn his head but he couldn't. Of course, this wasn't really happening. It was all in his mind. The witch could force him to see what she wanted.

"Go away!" Chase shouted as loudly as he could.

The door slammed open. A shadow lurked there.

The witch turned, startled.

Chase thought he saw fear in her eyes. Smelled something burnt.

Then she was gone.

Chase's eyes flew open. He still sat in his cellar, alone. The chill made gooseflesh rise on his arms.

He pulled up the blankets he'd been left, looking around.

His body felt lighter. It felt easier to be in his body. He had space in his mind. Room to think his own thoughts, feel his own feelings, not have to guard them against something other.

He felt as if he'd woken from a long illness and was just now finding out what he could do.

Chase wanted to run to the door and scream he was healed. Caution made him wait.

Too many tricks had been played on him. For all he knew, the frost witch might have just invited another of her kind into his mind. They might be lurking, waiting to jump out when he least expected it.

Chase sighed. He stood up, blanket wrapped around him, and began to pace. He'd taken to doing that so his body didn't get too soft. Sometimes he did pushups on the rug they'd given him, but mostly he just paced.

Things were changing. He needed to get his head in the game.

Drew sat in his favorite chair. His Kindle waited for him, but he had no desire to read. The adventures of a fictional character held no interest right now.

Chase's frost witch might have a link to him, a link forged when Drew had been healing after his resurrection. Not something he had control over.

No matter. It reinforced Drew's feeling that he was a danger to the clowder. The idea of jumping through the portal appealed to him. As a guardian, not a watcher, Drew didn't know how to program the portals. If he were going to jump through one into a dead space, he'd need help.

Matt and Anson weren't likely to help him. Chase might. If he did, Drew might be able to bring him through the portal with him, destroying Chase's frost witch as well as the two of them.

Though the clowder would be shattered at the loss of the two of them, they would understand that in the long run, it was for the best. The only issue Drew had was how to take Courtney with them.

Courtney had power, far more power than he did.

Perhaps even more power than Chase. Drew had no idea how to get Chase to help him, though. The frost witch inside Chase, the one that could jump into Drew, wasn't likely to let him go through the portal. Not if it thought it might need him.

Drew sat in his chair, his thoughts in turmoil.

He looked up at a knock on his door. His chair squeaked quietly when he leaned forward.

"Come in!" Drew said.

Kayley stood in the open door, carrying two mugs. Hot chocolate. He could smell it from there.

"Can you be here?" Drew asked. "Grey said..."

"Grey went upstairs after Courtney asked Grey about what happened after his species died. The cats are wondering if the frost witches are related to the people on Cat Home.," Kayley said. "You missed that."

The mug was warm in Drew's hands. He appreciated it. Outside the day had turned to a darker gray. It was too early for the sun to be setting, only mid-afternoon, but the sky was darker, the clouds hanging even lower than before. A good day for hot chocolate.

"How could Cat Home not know?" Drew asked.

Kayley shrugged. "We're still figuring it out."

"You're worried about sharing what you think," Drew said, hoping to draw her out.

"I feel like if the frost witches are from Cat Home and they were supposed to be dead, then what does that make us? Think about how the frost witches get magic. They get magic by taking life force. Do the cats do that? Is that why they need us? Do we feed them?"

Drew wondered what Kayley's big brown tabby, Elmore, was telling her.

"What does Elmore say?" Drew asked. He had an overwhelming urge to reach out to Mack right then. He missed the cat every moment of every day and always would, but in that instance, the ache of the loss of his telepathic bond reached a crescendo.

"He thinks it's true," Kayley said quietly. "He believes that the frost witches are related. There was a theory that they were. Everyone thought it was ridiculous, but now… it seems like it was right. And the cats know that they pull some life force for their magic, but they don't hunger for it like the frost witches. It's like someone taken over by a magical cancer."

Drew thought about that. Magical cancer.

"Can Amber treat it like cancer? Use the same herbs? We know garlic works." Drew tried to remember if Courtney was avoiding eating garlic.

"Courtney needs a lot of garlic and it doesn't get rid of the witch but sends it back into hiding. Maybe it's the garlic or maybe it's the discomfort. I remember Amber, Riley, Stuart, and I talking about it."

Kayley would have been included in those talks because she had medical training as an EMT. Stuart would have insisted upon all input. Even if he hadn't been cut off from Mack, Drew wouldn't have been included. He had no such training. His thoughts fell into a familiar pattern of feeling useless.

"What does that mean?" Drew finally asked, trying to parse what she was saying.

"Is it possible that something like garlic, that's already been pulled and is essentially dying, can make the creature uncomfortable, but doesn't provide enough life force for the witch to balance the discomfort?" Kayley asked. "Is there something similar we could try with Chase?"

Drew felt a crawling sensation on the back of his neck, and smelled something burnt, like a candle.

"I don't know," he said. "We could try it. You could try it

with me. I've been carrying garlic but it doesn't seem to make a difference in me. The shadows still come back. Amber hasn't even been removing them any longer."

Drew knew it was an experiment to see if more shadows showed up or if Drew maintained the same number. The shadows, though, were a link between him and the frost witch. He hated that.

The house creaked oddly, just the faintest sound, almost as if the furnace was about to come on, but it wasn't starting.

Drew frowned as he stood.

Kayley stood with him, her head turned.

"Elmore says Grey is hurrying down, practically flying. He wants to see Chase. He thinks something has happened. Elmore can't get a sense of what," Kayley said. "I should go."

Drew nodded. He'd stay there, in his room. Be useless alone.

When she left, leaving the door open a crack. Drew stared out at the falling snow, the individual flakes difficult to make out against the gray background. Even so, they were hypnotic.

Biting his lip, Drew went back to considering how to get through the portal with both Chase and Courtney.

Courtney stood in the kitchen, as far from Chase's basement prison as possible. She grabbed a Dr. Pepper from the refrigerator and sipped it, watching the others. Stuart had his head in his hands. Her questions bothered him.

She felt the cats upstairs, discussing the issue as well. Amber remained curled on the sofa. Her back was to Courtney so it was hard to make out what she might be thinking.

Courtney let her hands run across the pale granite countertop. She liked the cool, smooth sensation. Her frost witch pressed her to do something, to destroy something. It felt the frustration and shock that the household was feeling. It wasn't a favorite emotion to draw from—it preferred anger or sorrow—but it craved the energy of that emotion even so.

Soon enough the air changed. Grey was coming down the stairs. Courtney knew it was Grey because she detected no new scent in the room. The others in the clowder all had their unique smells. Even the cats smelled different to her now ultra-sensitive nose.

"What?" Stuart asked without looking up.

"I need to talk to Chase," Grey said.

Courtney watched Amber and Stuart get up to follow. Amber's body smelled of nervousness and concern. Stuart stank of downright fear. Courtney wondered if Grey had the same sensitive nose.

Tenny remained where she was. Kayley had already headed down the hallway to talk to Drew. No one had stopped her, probably thinking she wouldn't get close enough to let Chase's frost witch hop to Drew and then to her. Kayley was a fighter, unlike Amber.

Even so, the frost witch could make the hop if it wanted to. Courtney monitored the room, making sure she didn't feel anything changing. Of course, such a thing would set off the alarms in her little shield spell, so she'd know if the frost witch tried anything that big. She'd felt Chase's frost witch reaching for life force earlier, sipping a bit and then sneaking away.

It thought she didn't know. Courtney had decided to let it have its sips. If it didn't think she knew, it would be more careless when it tried to break out.

Courtney shivered. The creature used to do give her chills when she figured something out that it didn't want her to know. The witch hadn't done anything for nearly a month, not since she'd managed to cage it.

Grey didn't think the cage would hold.

She closed her eyes. Examined the bars.

All safe.

Her frost witch was in the cage. She didn't see it drawing energy.

Something was pulling energy from the frost witch and thus from her.

Courtney opened her eyes. Everything looked normal in the house.

She set her soda on the counter.

Tenny wasn't shivering.

"Something's happening," Courtney said.

"From downstairs?" Tenny asked. Her eyes were half-closed, no doubt sending information to her guardian cat, Boyd.

"I don't get a direction. Whatever it is, it's pulling energy from the creature inside me. Too much energy," Courtney said.

Her body felt weak. She tried to move but stumbled.

Tenny helped her to the stairs, acting as if nothing was happening. Only Courtney struggled.

Courtney and her frost witch.

Courtney pulled herself up to the second floor. Tenny stayed behind, to guard the first floor. Fortunately, the second floor stairs were right next to the first floor stairs and she could wrap her arms around the pole and turn around to keep climbing.

The cats peered at her from the library as she rounded the corner. While she was near them, she warmed, slightly. The burnt candle smell that their magic always left in its wake lingered.

For a few moments, Courtney felt energized enough to keep going. Her body shivered, but didn't shake.

Unfortunately, the magic didn't last. About halfway up, she started to shake. Then, a few steps from the top, she had to sit down and rest. Whatever magic the cats had done hadn't just worn off, something was destroying its effect.

Courtney's body shook harder. She breathed out. Fog appeared in front of her.

The house wasn't that cold. No one else had been shivering.

Courtney crawled the rest of the way up the stairs and rested near the edge. Someone would come out soon enough.

She wrapped her arms around herself, trying to stay seated. Almost immediately she flung them out to keep herself from tumbling back down the stairs. She'd never been so cold.

Courtney pulled herself further into the hallway so she didn't accidentally fall down the stairs.

Her eyes closed. A relief because her eyelids were so heavy.

"What's happening?" Courtney asked of her frost witch.

There was no answer. In her mind's eye, Courtney saw her witch laying across the cage in which she imprisoned her. She didn't seem to be moving. She certainly wasn't eating the energy that was flowing out of Courtney.

The only thing Courtney knew of that could devour energy so quickly were other frost witches. Witches plural came to mind, probably from the creature inside her. There were others out there and they had come to destroy her witch.

As she fell into a doze, not certain she'd ever wake up, Courtney wondered if frost witches destroyed their own, leaving only the strongest to continue devouring the life force of the worlds. That would be one good thing to come out of learning there were others. Maybe the clowder could find a way to turn them against each other.

She felt no answer from her frost witch.

Courtney was too tired to hope that the creature was dead… and she was free.

The stairs creaked under Grey's weight, though he often seemed to only partly be there, in the house. The structure knew he was there. The basement smelled of damp turning to mold. They'd pulled up the carpet but the subfloor was still airing out. Some of the boards had been replaced but it had been surprisingly hard to find people to work for them.

Amber knew that Base Command had gotten people to replace windows quickly. They appeared to be having a harder time with the basement, though she wasn't certain why.

The room was dark and gray with the hurricane shutters pulled across the windows. It was too bad there wasn't a way to see out and to bring in some natural light even when the shutters were closed. Normally, the lack of a window didn't bother her. She spent a great deal of time in her windowless office, but for some reason not having access to the outside in the big room bothered her.

The subfloor felt cool beneath her slippered feet. Amber wanted to jump back on the steps, which were still carpeted, where it was warmer. Both Grey and Stuart continued down, apparently not bothered by the chill of the floor.

"*Courtney is feeling cold as well,*" Minnett said. "*Very cold. Is it possible it is colder down there?*"

Anything was possible. Amber didn't feel that cold though. Normally, Courtney could keep herself warm no matter what. She harnessed the frost witch inside her and used that energy. If she was cold, something was going on.

Amber hurried to catch up with Stuart and Grey. Grey was already opening the door. Amber didn't interrupt him. Chase could be waiting.

Anson had pushed his chair aside and was waiting practically in the doorway of his room, keeping an eye on everyone. He said nothing to any of them, though he gave Amber a nod with a raised eyebrow.

Despite Anson's casualness, Amber had visions of Chase striking out at Grey, sending a swath of frosty air freezing Grey in place. She hung back in case her vision became reality.

Grey walked into the room easily. Stuart followed, perhaps a bit further back. Amber wondered if he had the same concern. Earlier, nothing had happened, but Chase had to be the reason Courtney was so cold. He, or his frost witch, was doing something.

Once she turned the corner into the room, Amber saw Chase sitting on the futon. He hadn't gotten up for them. Often he stood when they were there, his chain clanking against the cement floor. Stuart stood a few feet behind Grey. Amber waited near the edge of the door.

"More have come through, haven't they?" Chase asked. "I felt it. Felt the opening of the portal and felt three sentient beings drop through."

Normally the watcher cats were the ones who felt the portal open. The watchers picked up those echoes, but

Amber hadn't heard of any other watcher feeling the portals open once their cat had passed on. Of course, Trag hadn't passed on, no matter that he and Chase weren't bonded any longer

"He is right though," Minnett confirmed.

Grey said nothing. He didn't move. Even Stuart seemed fidgety in comparison to Grey. Just the other day, Amber would have described Stuart as unnaturally still. Courtney would have said vampire-like.

"What does the frost witch think?" Grey asked.

Amber kept her face neutral. She wouldn't have recognized talking to Chase versus the frost witch, but Grey did.

"We don't usually communicate," Chase said. "It lets me out except when people are here, usually. It really doesn't like you. It's almost afraid of you. I get the sense that they are fleeing something, something that found them on their last planet."

"Are there more coming?" Grey asked.

"I don't know. I'm not sure the frost witch does. Ask Courtney. She might get more from her frost witch."

"Courtney is upstairs. She's terribly cold. I believe she is under attack. We've tried to help but it wasn't enough," Minnett said.

Stuart's shoulders tensed along with the muscles around his hips. Trag must have sent him the same message. His first instinct would be to help Courtney. If Amber wasn't sure he was incapable of attachment, she'd have said he had a crush on Courtney.

"For the moment, Courtney is under attack," Grey said. He appeared calm. Of course, he didn't appear to care about individuals. They were nothing to him. Humans were like bugs.

Chase looked down. Even he looked more concerned than Grey acted.

"Is the creature inside you one of the ones sent into our sun?" Grey asked.

"I don't even know how to ask," Chase said. Then he was quiet. His head tilted. Everything about him stopped just for an instant, a movie film glitch as it paused.

"Yes," Chase said coming back. He didn't exactly sit the same. Amber couldn't have put her finger on the difference. Something about the set of his shoulders exuded confidence right then.

"How did you get out?" Grey asked. "The sun should have destroyed you."

"Nothing completely destroys us. The sun we escaped from was dying, before you left your original home and traveled to another planet to plunder," the frost witch inside Chase said. "We fed upon the energy of the burning light, bringing death to that star sooner than it would otherwise have come. Then we loosed ourselves upon the worlds."

Grey looked down. "And now you've returned."

"Not intentionally. Who knew where our kind had gone? There are those among us who would gladly feast upon those who were our undoing."

Amber shivered, watching Chase, who was clearly not Chase, speak.

"The others are feasting on one of their own. How do they expect to take me down if they fight among themselves?"

"The creature it inhabits has chained it. Changed it. Each world changes us but we come back to ourselves. This one would not. It must be destroyed, particularly as another hunts us. We will not battle on two fronts," Chase's creature said.

"And why aren't you changing while in this person?" Grey asked.

"I am more powerful than that one. And this creature is weak."

Chase did that still thing, the slight movie glitch as if the film caught, before he looked up again.

Amber turned to leave. She had to help Courtney. She'd learned what she could about the frost witches. She noticed Grey didn't ask about what hunted the frost witches. Maybe he didn't really care. He thought of each of them as insects.

She felt Stuart behind her when she reached the door. He followed close on her heels as she hurried to the stairwell. Turning to go up, Amber noted that Grey also followed. He didn't appear to hurry but his steps covered the basement floor more quickly than they should have.

Amber practically ran upstairs.

She might not completely trust Courtney, but she wasn't going to let the woman die on her watch, not if she could help it. Her job at the clowder was to keep people alive.

The third floor seemed impossibly far away, even as she took the stairs to the second floor. The cats were still in the library. Amber heard them purring. Felt the warmth surrounding her. Her breathlessness eased, her muscles moved easier, she felt better.

No doubt her legs moved a bit faster, her feet reached a bit further, taking the next set of stairs two at a time. Courtney was on her side in the middle of the hallway.

Cari had covered her with a blanket, and placed a pillow beneath her head. Courtney wasn't moving. Her chest rose only slightly, taking in barely enough air to keep her going.

Amber fell to her knees to assist. She had her eyes closed even as her hands went to Courtney's body. Like a swimmer diving into a pool after a drowning child, Amber plunged into Courtney's energetic field, noting that even the blackness that had spread through her body looked gray.

Courtney's body felt cold, not just against Amber's physical hands, but in the energetic world. Sinking deeper, the energy moved only sluggishly.

"You need to get out," Minnett told her. *"Send her energy if you must but don't stay in her energy field. They attack there."*

The communication stopped. Minnett returned to purring a strange sound that Amber felt in her head. She pulled out of the energy level and looked at Courtney's organs, sending energy to the heart and kidneys, the two main organs that would help keep her alive.

The coldness deepened. Amber couldn't feel her body. She swam back to the place she thought was the surface, but it was impossibly far away.

Minnett's mind touched hers, still purring. Amber followed the sound.

She pulled back into her physical body and opened her eyes. Stuart was on the other side of Courtney. He was sending deep golden energy into Courtney's body, his eyes only half-open.

Amber did the same, though her energy was a paler yellow, probably because she felt cold and tired. She'd probably compromised her ability to heal because she'd leaped into something too quickly. No matter that it felt like the right thing to do, she had to pause and assess, always. It was her job.

No one else said a word. Even Grey stood quietly, a hand held up, pure silver energy radiating it from it into Courtney's body, creating a web of sorts, a web that felt both protective and healing.

STUART

Amber might have leaped into the energetic fields, but Stuart paused to assess Courtney's situation. He had a sense of Amber swimming through energy that felt gray and sluggish as he examined Courtney. Stuart didn't have Amber's healing abilities. He could, however, send energy and it seemed to him that Courtney needed it.

He anchored himself with Trag, who was working with the other cats, creating their own magical spells. Stuart felt the enhanced energy in his own body. He hadn't been tired. Now he felt as if he'd drunk a few gallons of coffee.

"*A shield, if you can,*" Stuart thought.

Trag didn't answer with words. His mind was on holding the threads of a spell together. The frost witches would come through any shield they tried to put up.

Feeling the anchor, letting Trag know what he was about to do, Stuart pulled energy from the land and the air and started letting it flow into Courtney. He would still deplete some of his own energy but he could feed her a lot more than he could if he hadn't done those things.

The land felt dead. He had to reach more deeply into the ground to draw what he needed. The land had been recovering from the last time it had snowed but now it was once again back to minimal levels of life. It made him wonder if the frost witches were aware of how depleted the life force of the land got and they backed off so that it could recover. Doing so would prolong their feeding.

The idea didn't feel right. If they did that, they could leach off a planet for centuries, nearly destroying it and letting it come back. Stuart had the impression that frost witches were greedy. They were beings like the ones from Cat Home only without restraints. If the beings at Cat Home hadn't really known the frost witches had escaped the sun by eating it, it was no wonder there were no records there. Even if there were, Stuart wondered how much they would care so long as the witches didn't come to their home world.

The energy he fed Courtney faltered. Stuart had to bring his concentration back to healing.

The land beneath him became not just dead but practically desiccated. Nothing was there. No matter how deeply Stuart reached, no life existed. He'd felt it earlier. He reached out further, finding only the same thing, as if the entire world had died and he was there looking for energy.

Coming out of his healing trance, Stuart noted that Grey was drawing energy, large swaths of it that might wipe out the flora and fauna around the neighborhood for a generation. Then the drawing just stopped. Only Amber continued to give Courtney energy. She was drawing from the sun, but it was a tiny trickle compared to what he and Grey had given.

"I have created a shield to keep the other frost witches from attacking her," Grey said. "She'll be able to keep it up when she wakes. I expect she should be okay."

"You took most of the life force from the land beneath the

house. Half the neighborhood," Stuart said. "The trees will die…"

Grey said nothing. The absence of any understanding in his eyes made Stuart shudder internally. He couldn't give anything away to this creature.

"Her life is important right now. If she is not an ally to the frost witches, she can help us. I suspect their attack will make her entity more pliable once it gets back some of its energy," Grey said. "Someone should take her to her bed to let her rest. That's what humans do to heal, is it not?"

With that, Grey turned and walked down the hall to his room. He moved quickly, though he seemed relaxed.

Stuart touched Amber, who lifted her head. He noted that the trickle of energy stopped as quickly as she looked up.

"We should get her to her room and let her rest. Grey put a shield up around her and I think he fed her energy," Stuart said. He ought to have fed her energy given how much he took. Stuart felt sad for the trees and bushes that were going to die or come very close to dying. The neighborhood was a pleasant place to walk through when it wasn't snowing. The greenery drew him and the sounds of the water relaxed him. It would be a good place to live if he weren't tasked with finding and destroying the frost witches, and perhaps even destroying the clowder if that's what it took to stop the witches.

Amber stood up. She didn't wobble but she seemed less sturdy than she had running up the stairs. The cats continued to purr. It took only a moment for Amber to steady herself. Only then did Stuart feel he could bend and pick up Courtney.

She was heavier than he would have expected. Drew made carrying someone look easy. Stuart didn't have the other man's height or length of arm. He moved slowly. Cari opened the door to Courtney's room. The bed was turned down.

Stuart laid her on it. Cari got to work pulling off Courtney's slippers and tucking her in.

"Should we get food?" Amber asked.

"Probably," Stuart said. Food would help get her back on track. When Courtney sipped energy from the people in the clowder, they had all needed to eat. In fact, given the food bills, Stuart had a feeling she was still sneaking sips here and there. Everyone ate like they'd not had a meal in days now.

Everyone except Drew and Chase.

Courtney wouldn't be taking energy from either of them, but he couldn't be sure that the frost witch in Chase didn't take sips of Drew and siphon from Chase now and then. He filed that away. He'd ask Grey about that later. He'd only ask because it might give them another clue how to deal with these witches as well as the three that had just come through.

Stuart glanced up at the window in Courtney's room. The snow swirled down so hard he couldn't see out. Hopefully, the people of Lexington were staying safe and warm in their homes.

When Courtney opened her eyes she was in her field of dying flowers. They seemed less black and brown and deeper red than before. Nearly a month had passed since she'd landed there the last time. No sound reached her.

For the first time, she appeared to be on her back, looking up at the sky. A cloudless blue, it was as unchanging as the rest of the field. Courtney tried to remember how blue the sky had been before.

Thinking about sitting up, her viewpoint changed. In front of Courtney sat a figure that looked like her. Her hair was the same, slightly mussed blonde as if the figure had just sat up.

Courtney reached out a hand to touch. The figure reached out a hand also. Courtney noted that she, herself, had fingers. Normally she had no body in the field. This was different.

"I am here with you," the figure said.

"Who are you?" Courtney asked. Her voice sounded too

loud in the silence. Even so, she didn't feel the threat she normally felt.

"I am alive because of you," the figure said. "You call me the frost witch or the entity or the vampire."

"Why are we here?" Courtney asked.

"The one that you call Stuart thought this might be a place in your subconscious that allowed healing. He wasn't exactly right but he wasn't wrong, either. It is a mostly safe place for you in the non-physical world," the witch said.

Courtney had so many questions, she didn't know where to start.

The figure moved only when she did. "You see, I cannot move unless you do," the witch said.

"What should I call you?" Courtney asked.

The figure was silent for a long time. "It is long since I had a name. Longer than you could understand. Even your world, your Earth is not as old as I, and nothing has called me by name since before it was formed."

"Do you have a name you want to be called?" Courtney asked.

"What is easy for you to call me?"

Courtney thought about what she could call the witch. She ran through names that had vampire meanings like Elizabeth for the real Countess of Bathory, and then fictional vampire names like Lucy, Elena, and Bella. None of them fit this creature. The latter two, especially, were far too youthful.

"What about Dawn?" Courtney said. The name came to her from one of the vampire series books but it felt appropriate. This creature needed a new name and Dawn was new. This was a new thing for them.

"Then I am Dawn." The frost witch seemed to have no understanding of Courtney's cleverness which annoyed her.

"Why are we here? Besides the fact that it's safe? Why did we need a safe place?" Courtney asked.

"I nearly ceased to exist. I am only alive because of my links to you," Dawn said. "Your cage is no longer but you, what you are, as a human, is my cage now. If I were to leave, I could not survive. Somehow we have melded into one in our fight to survive."

Courtney wondered if Dawn could be killed and she would be freed.

"Do not think that you can extinguish me," Dawn said, clearly aware of her thoughts. "If I am gone, then you will die. You and I are stuck with each other though I find your sensibilities quaint and irritating and you find my hunger frightening. At this point, I can no more compel you to savor the lives of those around you than you could command one of the changeling cats."

"Changeling cats?" Courtney asked.

"The creatures that look like cats but were sired by my kind in that form long ago. Just as you are human but not human thanks to me, they are and are not cats," Dawn said.

"Why did you come here?" Courtney said. "Why did you want to destroy my world?"

"We were hungry," Dawn said. "It was finally a world with enough life force to keep us going for a few more eons. By the time we wore down your sun, the universes would have changed again and we would move on to another place." Courtney felt that there was more to be said but Dawn offered nothing else.

"I asked Grey about what you were. He hasn't yet responded," Courtney said.

"I know. He will have those of his kind, which were once my kind, looking for ways to destroy us. We need a very hot sun. I am not sure that even the full power of the new home planet they inhabit will be enough to drive all of us into it."

"Can't you just ask everyone to leave here?"

Dawn's long look told Courtney it was a stupid idea. "Why should I? Eating one world is as good as another."

Courtney was silent. She might have a truce with this creature, might actually spend more time in charge rather than trying to keep it contained, but she clearly didn't understand it.

"You will come to understand while we inhabit this body," Dawn said. "And you will inhabit it for a very long time."

The field warmed suddenly. Courtney closed her eyes to savor the moment. When she opened them, she was in her bed, the covers piled on. The light in the room as low. The sky outside held a gray so dark that it was nearly night. Courtney was pretty sure she hadn't been out for that long. Something about the angle of what light existed told her it was still late afternoon.

Now, she had to go out and find out what had happened to the rest of the clowder and what they might need her to do to get rid of the other frost witches.

She felt an agreement there, a rightness in her chest. Dawn didn't like the other frost witches either, probably because they had tried to destroy her. That might make life easier, at least for the moment. Courtney pushed herself up and put on her slippers, listening to the sounds around her.

The house felt too quiet. Worried she'd been out too long, Courtney hurried out to see what had happened while she healed in her field of dying flowers.

DREW

Kayley left to go back to her post to watch, leaving Drew alone in his room. Kayley had let him know that Grey hadn't harmed Chase. Drew felt relieved, which surprised him. He liked Chase as Chase. He hadn't liked him after the first snow. Like everyone else, he didn't trust him. It didn't really make sense that he was relieved that Grey hadn't hurt him.

Drew stretched and looked out the window, seeing nothing but gray and white. Even the trees were invisible. He might be living in a cloud. With all the shutters closed and the shields around the house, they might as well live in a cloud for all that people could get near them.

Walking out to the main room, Drew noticed Tenny pacing around.

"What's wrong?" Drew asked. He made sure to stay several feet away. If the frost witch in Chase jumped to him and then to Tenny, he didn't know how far away he needed to be to keep her safe. Perhaps he ought to go out to the covered patio downstairs.

"Something happened to Courtney," Tenny said. "She got

cold and then real weak. Amber and Stuart are up there with her."

The slight hesitation in between the names told Drew that Grey was probably there as well. It would be easy enough to destroy Courtney if he were. Probably for the best. At least the clowder wouldn't have to take on her death. They'd grieve, of course. Most people liked Courtney.

Drew couldn't quite make himself hurt her no matter that she threatened the clowder. Stuart threatened the clowder as Drew knew it as well, though at least Stuart had a reason to help them. Courtney's reasons were less certain. She acted like she wanted their help but she'd stayed home for a month between the first two big snowstorms. Then she'd appeared there and seemed to help them. To Drew, it didn't make sense.

"She's not dead," a voice whispered in his mind. *"You could try and kill her."*

He'd be a hero if he did. After all, it was Courtney who had brought the first frost witch. Or maybe it was Chase.

"Courtney," whispered a voice.

Drew started up the stairs. He met Stuart and Amber on the second floor.

"Where are you going?" Stuart asked. He held out a hand to stop Drew.

Drew considered pushing the hand away, pushing past and heading up to Courtney's bedroom but he paused.

"I needed to see Courtney," Drew said. That was honest enough. He knew Stuart wouldn't let him kill her. Stuart liked Courtney, perhaps a bit too much.

"She's resting," Amber said. "Let's go downstairs."

Amber made like she was going to take his arm, but Stuart held her back. They were more afraid of Drew than Courtney. That bothered him. She was the danger, not him.

Yes, he'd been dead and was brought back to life. If they

were worried about that, he'd understand but they kept looking for frost witch influence. He knew it was there. Chase had linked to him and talked to him telepathically. Drew heard Chase almost as clearly as he used to hear Mack. Still, he knew he hadn't changed that much. No frost witch tricked him into doing things.

"I'd rather see Courtney," Drew pressed. "I can watch her while she rests. Make sure that the frost witch doesn't come out. I'm probably more sensitive than most of you because of what happened."

Stuart shook his head. "I'll know if something goes wrong. So will Grey. Let's go downstairs."

Drew considered pushing the idea. Mack came to the door of the library and looked out. The big orange tabby stared at him, eyes slightly narrowed. It wasn't the round-eyed stare and slow blink that he used to give Drew. This was a suspicious stare, one that asked who he was.

Drew shook his head and then let himself be walked down the stairs.

He smelled burnt candle. The cats had done magic. He wanted to ask why the cats were doing magic, but other than Kayley, most of the clowder didn't trust him. Thankfully, Kayley kept him in the loop.

On the first floor, Drew paused at the stairs, looking up, wondering when he'd get back up there. Kayley watched him. Amber waited, gently touching his arm.

Amber jumped as if she'd been stung. Drew's eyes widened, as stunned as she was. He felt the cold electrical jolt between them.

Stuart came back and reached out to touch him. Drew shrank back, not wanting to feel the shock again. Still, Stuart continued reaching.

Another shock.

Stuart looked at his hand. Drew had no idea what he was

looking for. The narrowed, half-closed eyes suggested Stuart was looking at his energetic field.

Amber put her hand on Stuarts and closed her eyes. They were searching for something.

"You're clear," Amber said, looking at Stuart.

"As are you," Stuart said.

The two of them looked at Drew. He hadn't done anything. Hadn't intended to make them jump. He moved out of the way.

"I didn't mean anything. I didn't even try anything. I don't know what's going on!" He shrank away from everyone.

"Maybe Courtney can shield him when she wakes," Amber suggested.

Stuart gave a single nod. Drew wasn't certain what that meant. He left the room, walking down the hall to his bedroom. He could read in there, waiting until they did something.

Or he could plan what to do while he was there. His window overlooked the backyard, but with the walk-out basement, it was effectively on the second floor. He couldn't climb out. He could, however, go out the front door. He figured if he went out in a few minutes when only Kayley and Tenny were around, they'd be too late to stop him if he hurried.

Drew waited and listened. When he decided things were quiet enough, he got up. He tried to look natural walking out to the kitchen. Tenny was back in the breakfast nook. She was aware of him. Her eyes followed him to the kitchen.

The garage called to him, giving him a better idea than trying to rush the front door. There was a freezer in there, though they had several in the storage room where Chase was. The garage freezer had become the favorite since every-thing happened. It would be normal for him to go out there.

Drew acted like he was hungry, looking in the refrigerator and then the pantry. He looked over at Tenny before heading out to the garage. He waited a second but she wasn't following.

The garage was a huge thing with room enough for three cars. The freezer was in the third bay along with plywood, extra cat food, cases of soda as well as several bikes. Riley's car was in the garage along with Drew's.

For a moment he considered using his keys to drive away, but there would be other cars in the driveway. Everyone was parking as close to the house as possible, keeping cars off the street lest the neighbors decide to vandalize them.

He'd have to walk. Too bad he hadn't thought to bring a coat. Drew pressed the button for the garage door opener and hurried so that he'd be nearer the door when it raised enough. The sound would likely bring someone. Even if she didn't hear it, the cats would let Tenny know what was going on.

Outside Drew was confronted with what appeared to be a wall of pale gray. He took a breath and stepped into it, barely feeling it when someone or something grabbed onto his arm from behind.

STUART

Stuart looked in on Courtney before heading to his room. She was just down the hall. Her breathing appeared normal though she hadn't moved at all. The upstairs was quiet, almost too quiet as if the snow were damping the interior sounds.

Settling into his room to meditate and rebuild his energy, Stuart tamped down some impatience. Before, he'd been leading things, figuring things out. It had felt as if there weren't enough minutes in each hour to consider all the possibilities. Now that Grey was here, Stuart needed to take a backseat. Now it seemed like all he did was wait. He wondered if the clowder had felt that way about him.

Sliding down to the mattress that lay on the floor, Stuart prepared to make himself comfortable. The faint hiss of the furnace comforted him. The gray outside gave enough light for meditation. The mattress and the blankets kept him from feeling too chilled on the floor. The room held only a dresser in the corner, but for Stuart, that was enough.

Trag remained in the library. The cats had stopped trying to protect Courtney. They were building up the shield around the house, trying to keep magic out as well as people. Stuart lent his energy so they could strengthen it more. He didn't expect it would work that well. The frost witches were far more powerful. Chase had said something about three new ones.

That meant the clowder now faced five frost witches. Too bad Grey didn't know more about the total number of frost witches out there. Stuart sensed Grey was probably communicating with Cat Home to learn more about the estimates of how many of their kind might have been sent into the sun. From his visit there, Stuart got the sense that the species was not terribly fertile. To his knowledge, he'd not seen a single young one, which in hindsight seemed odd.

Funny how he hadn't questioned the fact before. There'd been no need. Cat Home stayed safely at Cat Home and he worked Base Command on Earth. His function had not been to work with them. That belonged to those at Base Command who had more authority and seniority than he did. At least with Grey here, no one was pushing him to destroy the clowder.

Stuart had made the argument that destroying the portal would be exactly what the frost witches wanted. With no specified portal, Base Command wouldn't be able to monitor their access to this world. For now, until Grey said otherwise, that action was on hold, which was a relief to Stuart. If he had to destroy the portal, he'd destroy the clowder as well as himself.

If the portal needed to be dismantled, perhaps Grey could do that. He would know how the portals were created.

"Drew is going outside," Trag told him. The speed of the communication, the force with which it pressed into his mind added urgency to the otherwise calmly delivered information.

Stuart was up and heading out his door before Trag's

voice was gone from his mind. Even then, Grey was already walking down the hall to the stairs, his strides moving him more quickly than they should. It was as if he teleported a few feet on each step, though Stuart didn't know how that was possible.

He hurried to catch up but didn't quite beat him to the stairs. Grey glided by him easily, not saying a word about why he might be wondering what Drew was doing.

"Why didn't someone stop him?" Stuart asked Trag.

Julia hurried out of her room. She was dressed in jeans and heavy boots. Coats were downstairs.

"He was in the garage. Tenny thought he was going for food. He'd been looking in the refrigerator moments before. It wasn't until she heard the door go up that she realized he might go out. She grabbed his arm before he was fully out there, but Drew managed to shake her off," Trag said. *"It was a near thing. She'd have held on, but Boyd made her stop. She'd have been dragged out into the snow otherwise."*

The snow changed people when they were out in it. Matt had had shadows in his energetic field when he'd come from being outside in the first snow. Amber had managed to heal him. The neighbors would attack the house after being in the snow. They'd even attacked the clowder when the others had gone out to pick up Matt in a respite during the first big snowfall.

They'd initially believed Chase had been infected when he went out in the first snowfall, but now it appeared that he'd been infected earlier. Still, he'd been changed in that snowfall, as the flakes had somehow strengthened the creature inside him.

They were joined on the second floor by Tom. Stuart figured Amber had headed down to her office in the basement.

Stuart paused at the coat closet and grabbed his coat. Cari

was just as fast. Tom right behind, an arm reaching over Cari's shoulder as she ducked out of the way. Behind them, Julia followed.

Kayley stood in the partly opened front door, looking out. The covered front porch would protect her from the snow. It had to be freezing though.

"Can you see anything?" Stuart asked. Grey had disappeared around the corner, probably going directly to the garage.

"No," Kayley said. "It's all gray. Like a wall."

Stuart paused to look over her shoulder. Kayley was shorter than he was and didn't block his vision. She was right. The porch was there but the snow fell so hard and the clouds were so thick and low that it looked like a gray wall beyond the cover of the porch. The shields had been set at the edge of the property, but he couldn't even see that far.

"The shields can't prevent snow," Trag said. *"If we could do that, we would. It would make life so much easier."*

Without Courtney, they couldn't even put up the shields they had. And even hers hadn't been particularly well made. She had strength, but didn't have the knowledge or experience to use it. It was only when Grey arrived that he'd tweaked the shield design so it was strong enough to keep the neighbors at bay.

His long coat on and buttoned, Stuart headed around the corner to the garage door.

"Can you see anything?" Stuart asked Trag.

"Pretty much the same gray wall as you see," Trag said.

Stuart wasn't surprised. He'd seen the same thing from his third floor bedroom in the back of the house.

The garage was freezing. Two cars sat in the spots closest to the door. Tenny was heading in to grab a coat. Grey stood at the edge of the garage, his feet neatly placed just behind the line of snow.

He stared into the grayness.

Matt already stood there, shivering and bouncing despite his coat. He must have gotten there just after Tenny.

"Anson is on watch downstairs," Matt said. "He didn't hear anything unusual from Chase."

Not that anyone would have heard anything. Sometimes it got cold down there when Chase worked magic, but he never made a sound.

"I do not sense anything beyond the wall. The witches may have cut us off in the same way we attempted to cut off the humans they influenced," Grey said. "I feel magic, though, and not just the snowfall."

Stuart waited. Grey would tell them when he was ready.

"The magic feels old. It has elements that we've long since stopped using. As much as I mislike the idea, I believe Courtney and Chase were telling us the truth about the origins of the frost witches."

Stuart hadn't doubted it. He had felt the truth of the statements deep down. Grey had to have as well, but perhaps he hadn't wanted to accept that truth.

"Cat Home says there were forty-four individuals sent to the dying sun. It had to have been painful to grab onto that energy to save themselves but there are those that would. Not all would have survived such an attempt. Not all would want to, for to fail halfway through would have been a destruction worse than not trying at all." Grey didn't move to look at anyone. Instead, he continued to stare out into the grayness.

Stuart stared as well. Matt stood to one side. Tom stood on Matt's other side. All watched, perhaps hoping Drew would stumble back towards them.

"I could go out with an umbrella and ski gear," Matt said. He'd closed some of the shutters one other time doing that.

"It could be easy to get turned around," Tom said.

"Tie a rope around my waist," Matt pressed.

"Drew couldn't have gone far if he didn't have a coat," Tenny said from behind them. Stuart turned. She was dressed in a heavy coat. She didn't look happy. Knowing Tenny, she took it personally that Drew had escaped on her watch, even though they were watching against someone coming in, not one of their own leaving.

"I believe such a risk is worth taking," Grey said.

Matt didn't wait for an argument. He hurried out of the garage to get his stuff. Stuart didn't like it. They could be down two people.

He was freezing in the garage despite his coat. He wondered what the temperature had dropped down to.

"Only the most demented of the old ones would have survived being thrust into the sun. They would have the most power and the fewest morals, even by the standards of my kind, which is so different from yours," Grey said.

It was the most human thing Stuart had heard from Grey. Stuart's fingers tingled in his gloves and he stuck them under his armpits while he waited for Matt.

CHASE

Chase laid down and closed his eyes. It took only a moment and he was at his lake. Courtney talked about a field of dying flowers. Chase had the lake, when he had anything. It was his favorite place his consciousness went when the frost witch took over.

No sounds had come through the walls suggesting someone was going to enter the room. No smells of perfume or body wash reached his nose. The very lack of anyone around had been the reason Chase laid down in the first place. He'd expected to dose, something he'd done a fair amount of in the last month.

Instead of sleeping and normal dreams, he was at his lake, which was a large oval with several inlets. Deep blue water suggested a fair amount of depth in the center with the color lightening as it got closer to shores lined in golden sand and sometimes small round rocks. Evergreen trees edged the beach on the far side.

Chase always sat in a four bench rowboat, the outside painted white, the inside polished wood. If he got close he smelled the scent of varnish as if it had just been done.

Nothing about the boat or lake reminded him of anything in his life. He could pick up a fishing rod, listen to the clink against the wood, the whir of the reel. Now and then he'd hear the plink of water when a fish surfaced.

He'd yet to catch anything while he fished. Of course, catching something wasn't really the purpose. It gave him something to do, a place to meditate.

Chase knew that Courtney's field wasn't nearly as nice. His frost witch had told him, had threatened him with the inability to smell or hear or use even a sort of psychic avatar while he fished in this psychic non-world.

Courtney's path differed from his in so many ways.

The fishing rod felt unnaturally heavy in his arms. Chase didn't understand why. The lake also felt colder than normal. Sitting there in the boat, he watched as fog rose up around him. Fog hadn't appeared on his lake before.

Chase started to get uncomfortable. Instead of fishing, he put the rod back down.

"What's going on?" he asked. He didn't mean to speak out loud. He waited for an echo but his voice seemed to be swallowed up in the fog.

"There are things to be done that require the energy of this place," a hollow voice told him. Normally Chase saw his frost witch as looking like Courtney, a very sexy Courtney. Its voice tended to mimic Courtney's, but this time the voice was so hollow that he couldn't have put a sex on it if he tried.

It gave Chase the chills. He closed his eyes against the fog. Someone had told him Courtney focused on her body when she came back. Chase focused on his body, hoping to take it back. Whatever was going on, the frost witch needed a lot of power. He'd been under the impression that holding that place for him didn't use much, was as effortless as breathing was for him.

Chase tried to imagine his body. He pictured the basement. It had been so long since he'd had much of a mirror, it was hard to picture how he looked. In his imagination, his body had become a boney skeleton from lying around barely eating. He focused on his hands. Courtney did that too. He didn't know why she did. He chose hands because he saw them regularly.

He imagined his fingers moving and picking something up. Tapping on his chest. He tried to tell himself he felt the movement on his chest.

His fingers got cold. They looked purple in his imagination. Chase's body felt frozen in place. He saw it, wrapped in a layer of ice, the comforter the clowder had given him wrapped around him.

Chase opened his eyes, expecting to see the lake. Instead, he was in the basement, lying on the narrow bed. He really was encased in a thin layer of ice.

His heart rate soared.

Chase tried to draw a breath but what air had been in the bubble was gone. He tried to raise his arm. The comforter snagged on him.

Pulling as hard as he could, finally, it moved. The ice cracked.

Chase punched through the ice in front of his face so he could breathe.

Gasping, he lay there. The frost witch needed him to survive.

Chase felt around, looking for her. He couldn't find her inside him. He felt almost normal, if you could call laying on a bed surrounded by ice normal.

Every time he moved his body, the pieces of ice broke off and fell to the ground. Chase was certain the frost witch had left him, at least for that moment.

He stood up and shuffled to the door. The chain around his ankle didn't quite reach. He moved back and sat on the bed, thinking. If the witch left him, it had to be important. Either something had happened to drive them off or the witch had gathered enough power that she didn't need him any longer.

Chase shuddered, hoping it was the former but terrified that it was likely the latter.

Courtney padded down the hallway. She listed at Cari and Julia's door but heard nothing. She took a long sniff outside the door. Both women were gone, their scent guiding her downstairs. From below, she heard the faintest creak of wood. Someone moved.

Not being alone calmed her. The lack of people on the third floor was normal.

Courtney went down to the second floor. She looked in the library. She smelled Riley. Heard her chair squeak.

The bond-mate cats looked at her, a dozen sets of eyes, watching. One of the black watcher cats, probably Navy, turned to look back out the window. Outside was nothing but a gray wall.

She turned to go down the stairs. She heard squeaks and perhaps groans from Riley's chair and knew she was getting up. Courtney had no desire to talk to her. Riley might know things, but it didn't matter. Courtney knew more, for now. Dawn would tell her what she needed to know.

On the first floor, the house felt colder than it should.

Kayley paced between the front room and the main room of the house. The door to the garage was cracked open.

Courtney heard voices. She smelled others out there. Tom, Stuart, Cari, and Fin. Fin's spicy cardamom-like smell was the strongest. He'd gone out last.

Courtney shivered. She went back to the coat closet and got her coat. She hoped her feet would stay warm enough in her slippers. She had no desire to go back upstairs to get her shoes.

"*We will stay warm,*" Dawn's voice whispered to her.

Pushing her arms through the sleeves, Courtney walked back through the great room.

"Drew is gone," Tenny said. She looked down at the island counter where she stood.

Courtney got an image of Drew leaving through the big open garage door, the double door, not the single in the corner, and walking into the gray wall, disappearing even as Tenny grabbed onto his arm.

Dawn felt Drew out there, smelled him.

Courtney would be safe enough going out to rescue him.

"I'll get him," Courtney said quietly.

Tenny looked up at her. Courtney couldn't read the expression on her face. It might have been hope or perhaps shame that Tenny hadn't been able to stop him from leaving.

"You don't read minds," Courtney said. "I sort of can." Sort of was right. She sometimes read minds. Sometimes nothing came through.

Her comment didn't seem to make Tenny feel any better. Instead of trying to find the right words, Courtney went out to the garage. She expected to get colder, but she didn't. Dawn was right. She did feel the sense of taking in life force which made the temperature drop even lower around her, but her body temperature remained comfortable if a bit cool.

For once, she wished she understood physics a bit better so she understood how things worked.

Courtney walked to the edge of the door. She noted that Grey had his feet lined up right along the edge of where the bare pavement ended and the snow-covered pavement began. Another fraction of an inch and he'd be touched by the snow.

"I'll get him. He's not far," Courtney said, talking about Drew. Grey would know that.

She put up her hood, mostly so her head would stay warmer. Dawn didn't seem to have an opinion. Courtney marched out through the snow. Before the wall, the driveway had been covered in less than an inch. Beyond the wall, there was nearly a foot of the stuff.

Her feet got soaked in moments. Courtney didn't feel it. She ran her hands along the edge of her little car, which was parked closest to the garage now. It was next to Julia's Subaru. Sniffing the air, Courtney thought Drew was only a few feet beyond her car.

She walked on. She had about an arm's length of visibility. The snow was falling harder than she'd ever seen it. Flakes didn't swirl or whirl in corkscrew patterns. They flew at her face and at the ground, ready to punch through the land.

Courtney was aware of force.

Drew was curled on his side just behind her car. He hadn't passed through the little shield she had put up. Courtney felt the magic, felt how weak it was. The shield wasn't a barrier, merely a small warning.

She knew the other frost witches were out there.

Courtney tried to get Drew to stand, but didn't have the strength. Dawn helped her, pushing him up using magic. Courtney dragged him toward the garage, his body an inch or so above the snow. A finger slumped over and drew a line in the fallen snow as Courtney pulled.

She passed the front of her car when something shimmered behind Drew.

Dawn pressed her to hurry. Courtney felt herself moving faster even before Dawn's urging. The frost witch could control her body when needed.

The other frost witches had arrived at the house. Nothing had happened beyond the slight shimmer in the air, but Courtney knew. She felt them. Sounds echoed in her head, words that she didn't quite understand and Dawn didn't bother to translate. Felt the disgust at what she had become, the desire born of something like fear that required she be destroyed.

Courtney reached the barrier with Drew.

She turned, putting her body between Drew and the witches, walking backward. A huge hand, the size of a bear, reached out through the gray wall, towards Courtney.

Vaguely she saw Grey throw up his hands, sending a bolt of magic arching towards the hand.

Courtney felt Dawn wrap a shield of ice around her, grounding her feet deep into the lifeless earth beneath the garage.

Even Stuart threw up a small shield, his puny in size compared to Dawn's and Grey's.

The hand didn't back up. It continued reaching. It wasn't going after Stuart or Grey or even Tom or Cari.

"It wants us," Dawn said.

With a thought, Courtney drew life force from those around her, not too much, but enough to warm the air around the hand, enough to make it start to melt.

Grey began to pull life force from the neighborhood. Courtney felt it, felt him pulling it from the neighbors, from the homes that adjoined their neighborhood and then he too warmed the hand, melting it further.

A finger broke off after a few seconds. Courtney lit the rest of the hand on fire.

It withdrew into the gray wall.

At her feet, Drew lay still. She didn't even see his chest rising and falling. Courtney didn't know if it was cold enough to kill him that quickly or not.

STUART

Stuart stood in the cold garage shivering when Courtney pulled Drew into the space, followed by a giant hand. The hand itself seemed to draw magic from him. Stuart threw up a shield, but for him and for those around him.

Magic shimmered around Grey as he did his own shielding. Stuart felt Grey's magic searching for the origins of the hand. For Stuart, the sense of the hand disappeared at the gray wall.

Courtney turned and added her magic to Grey's. The hand began to melt. Stuart felt the heat reach him. Grey's magic smelled like burnt candles. Courtney's smelled like a distant bonfire.

Grey added his magic to Courtney's. The hand began to melt faster, a small flame lighting in the palm of the frozen thing, and then it was just gone.

Stuart knelt near Drew.

"Tell Amber to be ready," Stuart told Trag.

"She's aware," Trag said. *"Already in the medic room powering up the heat lamp."*

Stuart had already picked up Courtney once. He wasn't sure he was up to carrying someone else, particularly not someone as large as Drew. Matt, Tom, and Fin each took a limb and lifted Drew's body. They slowly, awkwardly, made their way between the cars in the garage.

Stuart watched. He winced as he heard a bang against the door, worried it was Drew's head, but it seemed to be his foot.

"I didn't see him breathing," Courtney said. She wrapped her arms around herself. It didn't seem as if she were cold, though her pajama bottoms were soaked as were her slippers.

"You might want to go in and warm up," Stuart said gently.

"I'm fine," Courtney replied. She looked back out at the gray wall.

Stuart didn't like it. Didn't like the feeling.

"*They're out there,*" Trag whispered. "*We theorize that perhaps they led Drew outside so that Courtney would leave the safety of the house and her shields.*"

"I didn't go beyond the house shields," Courtney said.

Stuart gave her a long look. Clearly, she heard Trag.

"They were weak compared to this wall," she continued.

"They had time to examine you," Grey said. "Time to see what's going on inside you. Your essence feels more like my own than even Stuart's."

Stuart stilled. Interesting. For some time Courtney's energy had felt rather like the energies of those at Base Command but she had felt more human than any of them. Now, though, Grey was right. She felt more inhuman than even the oldest of the workers at Base Command.

"When they attacked earlier, Dawn and I became one," Courtney said.

"Dawn?" Stuart asked. Grey's expression didn't change,

but his eyes moved from Courtney to Stuart. He shouldn't have said a word.

"The frost witch. I asked her name. She didn't remember so I gave her one," Courtney said.

"She made the last shield you put up, didn't she?" Grey said.

"I guess?" Courtney said. "It's not like we're really separate any longer."

"You haven't been really separate entities for some time," Grey said. "Now you're just working together rather than at odds. She knows she'll be destroyed if the other witches catch her. They can't abide weakness."

Stuart said nothing. Base Command hated weakness, too, though they wouldn't admit their own. Did the frost witches prey upon each other if they sensed weakness? Was that part of what tore apart other worlds—petty bickering amongst themselves, trying to gather the greatest amount of life force?

Grey said nothing. He turned back to the cold. He wasn't as warmly dressed as Stuart but he didn't seem any more affected by the cold than Courtney was. Stuart's entire body shook and he had to move back further into the garage. Cari joined him, also too cold.

"Should I close the main door?" she asked.

Stuart shook his head. Warmth flooded from the partly open door in the house. He knew he ought to pull it closed but he needed it to remain outside. They were all waiting for something.

The air was still, as if a storm was coming in. Stuart listened.

He heard the slightest whistle of sound. He couldn't place what it was like. Maybe a wheeze. The hand reappeared and grabbed Courtney around the waist.

Courtney struggled.

Stuart watched as Grey threw fire at the hand, near the wrist.

It pulled back, still holding Courtney as she struggled against the hand.

Laughter echoed around the garage.

Pain lanced through Sutart's head. He felt the shields he'd left in place around Chase, down in the basement, break open and disintegrate. Stuart felt as if he were attached to those shields, an ache hammering through his head, forcing him to close his eyes and bring up his hands. As quickly as it came on, the pain faded.

The pain had lasted long enough, though, that not only was Courtney missing, but so was Grey.

Amber hurried into the medic room when Minnett let her know they were bringing Drew down. The lights were bright against the white vinyl floors and white cabinets. Three massage tables sat in the room, one after the other, giving people just enough space to walk around each one without brushing into the table behind. All had hydraulic lifts so that they could be raised or lowered once the patient was comfortable. The head or knees could be raised separately for comfort.

Table warmers wrapped each of the tables under flannel sheets. Amber turned the warmer on the nearest table, setting it to high. She turned on the far-infrared heat lamp as well. From the upper cabinets, she pulled out a box of needles and set it on the counter.

From a drawer in the lower cabinet, she pulled out a partly burned stick of moxa. Shaped like a cigar, moxa was a pressed herb that would warm areas of the body. It was also very smoky. Unfortunately, she didn't use a lot of loose moxa, which tended to be even smokier, but would have warmed Drew more quickly. She put the moxa back.

"*How is he?*" Amber asked Minnett, through their telepathic bond. Though none of the cats were there, they would know what was going on.

"*He's completely out,*" Minnett said. "*I'm on my way down.*"

Amber hated that Minnett would be so close to the room where Chase was imprisoned. They'd been trying to keep the cats away from him, but if Drew were hurt badly, Amber would need Minnett to help her with healing. Ideally, Grey would help, too, though Amber wasn't sure she'd trust him.

Minnett bounced into the room. Beyond, Amber heard several people moving down the stairs. They were moving slowly and awkwardly. Several people clearly had to carry Drew.

"*Grey and Courtney have disappeared,*" Minnett reported.

"What?" Amber demanded, out loud. Courtney would have backed her up with power, if necessary. While she wasn't always in control of her power, Courtney was very good about lending what she could when necessary.

Minnett hopped up onto the counter near the needles. "*Cari said a large icy hand grabbed them and was gone. They'd battled it earlier, but it came back after Drew was removed from the garage. It just grabbed them. The shields around Chase are completely gone, so no doubt he had something to do with the disappearance.*"

"You shouldn't be here, then," Amber said. She rested a hand on the cat's head. She knew firsthand what the frost witches could do to the cats.

"*Drew is near death,*" Minnett said. "*I can feel it from here. You need me.*"

Minnett was right. Amber could work with the cat from a distance but it was always better when Minnett was right there.

"What about Stuart?" Amber asked. Her voice was barely heard over someone swearing on the stairs. Drew was a big guy. He was heavy, too, which meant the people carrying him would be struggling. The stairs weren't that wide, either.

"When the shields came down, he was in a great deal of pain," Minnett said. *"Trag says he's getting better now. For the moment, he's still in the garage with Cari and Tenny. They are trying to figure out how to search for Grey and Courtney."*

Amber wasn't sure that searching for Grey and Courtney was a priority over a man's life, but Stuart wasn't absolutely necessary to the healing.

Tom walked backward into the room. He had Drew's upper body. Fin and Matt had a leg each. No doubt coming down the stairs had been a challenge. Amber couldn't picture how it would have been done.

She gestured to the first table, which was down as low as it would go. Relief spread across the men's faces as they laid Drew down. Amber raised the table. Drew's chest rose and fell, though only shallowly. His skin was almost as pale as it had been when he'd died.

With the table at the height she needed, Amber pulled the heat lamp over Drew's belly to warm his core.

"Find a blanket and wrap his feet in it," Amber ordered. "Then get another one to cover him."

Matt went to find blankets. Tom and Fin helped Amber strip Drew down to his underwear. For the moment his clothing wasn't wet, but ice had formed on his shirt and pants and as it melted, the dampness would keep the heat from warming him up as quickly as they needed.

Amber felt Drew's pulses. They were slow and sluggish, but they were there. Heat was the most important thing.

Minnett leaped over to the table, staying near Drew's head. Matt had a blue fleece blanket that he laid over Drew. He wrapped a darker blue one around Drew's feet.

Amber watched as Minnett stepped gently onto Drew's chest and extended her claws. Amber placed a hand on

Drew's chest, carefully avoiding the heat lamp. She closed her eyes and looked at his energetic body.

Shadows lurked around his organs as if an energetic sun shone down on them. Amber pulled at the darkness, wishing she'd thought to ask for a jar to place the dark energy into.

Someone touched her hand with a cool glass. Minnett had probably sent a message to the cats. While Amber was aware of her cat, could see Minnett's energies helping her own, she didn't exactly hear her the way she did at other times.

Amber moved in closer. In Matt and Chase, shadows had wrapped themselves around the spine. A few shadows were hovering near Drew's spine, but none had wrapped themselves around it. Amber pulled those out. The shadows moved like cotton candy, stretching and thinning as she pulled. Still, like cotton candy, she was able to get most of it off.

She went back and pulled the smaller hair-like strands when she finished.

Once his organs looked clear, Amber sank down into his energetic field. She felt the chill in there. Every energetic field looked different. Drew's was empty. It wasn't dark or light, just nothingness. Amber slipped back into the field closer to his physical body. He was alive. She saw his organs working. There was energy in his physical body, but she found nothing on the spiritual plane.

"*I don't understand,*" Amber thought to Minnett.

"*Nor do I. I have not seen such a thing before, nor is there anything in my memories. I have more than usual thanks to Grey's visit. Normally, this would mean he was dead. The psychic energetic field was emptier than usual after he died but there was something,*" Minnett said.

Amber didn't like it. Was Drew really there? Of course, the frost witches manifested even in Courtney and Chase's energetic field. What worried Amber was that part of Drew was dead even if his body was alive.

She wished that she had someone to ask, someone who knew more.

Amber pulled out of Drew's energetic body and watched him breathe. Minnett pulled out as well, though Amber noted the cat sent a bit of energy into the body to help Drew heal. Amber wasn't sure that would do any good if Drew's spirit was gone.

Tom put a lid on the final jar and set it aside. Amber noted there were four jars on the counter, neatly lined up. It was too bad she didn't know if that would make any difference at all.

The reappearance of the hand surprised Courtney but not Dawn. Courtney had wanted to believe that they'd hurt the frost witches but Dawn had been waiting for their next move. When the giant ice hand returned and grabbed both Courtney and Grey, Dawn didn't seem particularly worried, which comforted Courtney a little.

The hand swept Grey and Courtney out of the garage and into the air. Despite Dawn's ability to keep her warm, Courtney felt the chill of the air as they flew a few feet above the ground. Courtney's hair whipped around her face making her wish she was someone who pulled her hair back every day.

When Courtney lifted a hand to wipe her face, it came back with traces of pink. Icy tendrils of hair had scratched her face.

The grayness eased past the wall around the clowder house, but the day still wasn't bright. Heavy clouds and snow kept visibility to a minimum.

The hand didn't crush them, though it could have. The

moment Courtney wondered why, Dawn supplied the fact that although their body would be damaged enough that they wouldn't be able to heal themselves, Grey wouldn't be destroyed. In fact, depending upon the ways Grey naturally used magic, he might be freer to do so without a body.

Apparently, everyone used magic differently. Courtney felt like Dawn's font of information was flowing so quickly that she could barely keep up with all she was learning.

The hand set them down in the park, not far from the portal. The ride had gone on longer than it should have to travel that distance, at least at the speed they were traveling.

Dawn wondered if the lengthy ride to a nearby place meant the frost witches were vying for control over what was to be done.

On the ground, the portal was as visible to Courtney's eyes as the clowder house door. It was a large archway of brilliant green with a light so bright beyond the arch that Courtney couldn't look directly through the portal.

Next to her, Grey drew himself up. Magic flowed around him in a brilliant orange light. The plants, dormant beneath the snow, seemed to wilt further. Courtney felt the life force being drawn out of them and into Grey.

Not sure what else to do, Courtney studied the portal. She'd been in the park before, even after she'd been possessed by Dawn, but this was the first time she'd seen the portal. Dawn let Courtney know that Chase didn't see the portal unless it was in use, which it wasn't at that moment. The cats would see what she saw, or something very close. Power radiated it from it, startling her.

Four figures apparently made of ice appeared in front of her. Unlike when Courtney had seen Dawn the first few times, these figures never became human figures. They remained humanoid in form but didn't actually appear to be flesh. Sexless and with only hints at eyes and a mouth, they stood about the same height as Grey and a bit taller than Courtney.

Courtney felt Dawn drawing magic though she didn't draw as much as Grey had. Courtney backed up a step. Dawn was nervous.

"You were one of us," the frost witches said clearly speaking to Courtney and Dawn. "We cast you out."

Not a single one of them raised a hand but Courtney felt them pulling life energy from her. Dawn snapped shields in place. The pulling continued. Courtney closed her eyes, examining their efforts. They were trying to pull her magic out of her.

Once, she might have let them, thinking it would take Dawn. Now she understood that Dawn was all that stood between her and death.

The frost witches stood off to the side of the portal. It held life force, lots of it. From Dawn, Courtney understood that the portal pulled small amounts of life force from the park and people around it. The amounts were minuscule, but having skimmed from the land and people for hundreds of years, the pool of energy was humongous. Courtney wished she had known about that pool sooner. She'd have gathered life force from the portal.

"Take too much and the portal will be destroyed, along with the clowder house and much of this land," Dawn whispered.

Courtney had a sense of what was too much, but she couldn't have given it an exact measure.

The frost witches were drawing what they could from Courtney, despite her shields. She closed her eyes and warmed the temperature around the park. Just enough to create rain instead of snow.

The ice figures looked at the moisture and then back at Courtney. They weren't pleased.

Frost hit Courtney, trapping her for a moment. Without a thought, she broke through it, moving her hands and arms.

The ground beneath her began to sink. Courtney tried to step away but her feet were trapped.

The icy figures appeared to be smiling.

Courtney stopped sinking. The mud trapping her feet broke apart. Dawn had caused the temperature to drop low enough that the frozen ground could be chipped away. Courtney stepped out.

Hardly daring to think, she rushed the nearest of the figures, the one that reminded her of Chase's stance. It was probably the witch that had been in him.

Courtney flung herself at the ice figure.

Cold wrapped around her, but nothing she couldn't handle.

Her body landed on the hard ground. The figure beneath her shattered, silently, into a million pieces. The faintest bluish-white smoke drifted away from the figure and disappeared from the park.

Courtney sat up. Grey wasn't looking at her. He was looking at the other three frost witches.

Since everyone was ignoring her, Courtney threw herself at the next witch. Instead of the creature falling down, Courtney felt as if she'd run into an icy cold brick wall. Her entire side throbbed in pain.

The figure didn't even glance at her.

The rain turned back to snow.

STUART

Stuart stared out at the snow falling. The grayness hid any hint of where the hand might have taken Grey and Courtney.

"Base Command has had contact with Grey," Trag said. *"He and Courtney have been taken by four frost witches."*

Stuart lingered over the word four. Courtney had told them there were three more. The shields had broken, so Chase's frost witch could be with them.

He didn't think the clowder could just leave Grey. Grey and Courtney were the only two that could possibly help them.

"Can Cat Home bring over anyone else?" Stuart asked. The portals moved but sometimes they moved slowly. It might be possible, though deep down he knew it would be foolish.

"Not directly to this portal. Several people from Cat Home will be jumping through four different worlds to get here as soon as possible. They have already determined their jumps. Another group will be arriving in Paris in about eight hours our time," Trag said.

Hoping from portal to portal took time. It also sapped

strength, even for natives of Cat Home. Paris was far too far away for anyone to get there in a reasonable amount of time.

"They are shape changers," Trag said. *"They don't have to take a shape we understand."*

Stuart got an image of a leviathan creature swimming beneath the waves. Of course. They would know that it was too far to fly, or perhaps they worried that a creature large enough to make the flight would be spotted and challenged. It would be much easier to swim across the ocean and not be noticed. Closer in, they could change into a more common earth creature.

Still, even eight hours might be too long.

He paced in front of the open door. Cari had moved back, closer to the cars.

"Can we suit up and drive over to the park?" Cari asked. "If we all have umbrellas we might be safe. It's not like there's any wind."

There was never any wind when the frost witches turned up. The wind was energy and they took it, just like they took everything else.

"How is Drew?" Stuart thought to Trag.

"Alive. Amber has him warming up. She is puzzled. His psychic energy field is empty. His organs are working and he appears alive, though."

Stuart didn't know what that meant.

"It is possible that a frost witch could take over someone who has no psychic field," Trag said.

Stuart worried there was another frost witch around. Turning to Cari, he considered her idea about driving to the park.

"It's a good idea," Stuart said to Cari. Alone, the group wouldn't be very formidable, but together, perhaps they could be. They'd have to bring the cats. In the house, they were a fortress. He hated to leave, but they couldn't leave their friends in danger.

"But I need to check on Chase and Drew first," Stuart told Cari as he turned to leave.

"We'll take Julia's car. It can seat five easily with the cats," Cari said.

Julia would drive and Cari would insist upon going. They'd want Tom and Tenny and himself. Matt, Fin, and Anson would have to stay behind. They needed someone to remain in the house besides Riley and Amber, but Stuart wished a watcher could join them. Each person had different strengths.

Stuart hurried inside, his body relaxing slightly as he reached the warmth of the kitchen. He didn't remove his coat, just ran down the basement stairs. He sensed Amber in the medic room with Drew. So was Tom. Anson was alone outside Chase's door.

"Anything?" Stuart asked. Despite the cool in the basement, he unbuttoned his coat.

Anson shook his head. "The cats say the shields are down, but Chase hasn't tried anything."

Stuart opened the door and looked in. Just as he did so, Chase bent over double, as if in pain. His hands flew to his head. Stuart heard the slap of them against the sides of his head.

Chase's body flailed, twisting and turning. The chain rattled on the floor hard enough that Stuart noted the strain. They'd need a new one if they had to keep him in the basement.

Just as quickly as it had begun, the flailing stopped. Chase looked up, completely at ease. His hair was messed from his hands, but other than that, he might have been waiting for their arrival.

"I suppose you want to know how I got out," the frost

witch in Chase said. "I could have done it sooner, but it was more fun to wait for friends."

"Why are you back?" Stuart asked.

"To destroy you, of course," it said. Chase lifted his hand.

Stuart quickly raised a shield. He heard Trag and the cats purr at a shielding level, smelled the burnt candle smell.

Even so, he worried that their intervention would be too late for him and Anson.

DREW

Drew remembered walking outside the gray wall that surrounded the clowder house. His hand had touched the side of Julia's Subaru, buried beneath a layer of snow at least a foot deep, and he'd realized he was an idiot. His feet had kept walking. To stop would have meant falling down in the cold.

No wind ripped at his clothing. The cold was just there, an icy fist painfully squeezing air out of his lungs. His joints had ached and stiffened, just that quickly.

Drew had planned to turn around behind Courtney's car. He'd even wrapped his hands under his armpits, but he'd tripped on something, or maybe his knees had given out, the joints unable to take the cold air any longer. He hadn't dressed for a trip outside.

He'd felt nothing landing on the snow-covered cement of the driveway. This death wouldn't be as quick as the last one, but it wouldn't hurt. Drew realized he wasn't afraid to die. He'd been dead before.

Now though, his limbs burned. He inhaled warm air. His

lungs, used to the cold, ached with it. Maybe he'd gone to hell this time.

Drew's eyes flickered open. He noted the orange light of the heat lamp, realized the warmth making his joints ache was probably the table warmer, which Amber would have set on high. Blankets wrapped him.

"You're awake," Amber said quietly. "What were you thinking?"

Drew closed his eyes against the questions. He didn't remember what he'd thought. Then it came to him. "Grey said I was dangerous."

No more than that. He didn't intend to tell her he was heading to the portal to send himself through. He hadn't really had a good plan. He'd needed a watcher and a watcher cat to send him through to a place he wouldn't endanger anyone. Instead, he'd just wandered out into the snow.

Drew imagined Amber watching him as she thought about how to respond. "Chase is dangerous. Grey was being proactive. It didn't mean you had run outside and freeze yourself to death."

Drew's chest tightened against the deep ache inside. His eyes still felt dry. He couldn't cry, though his body demanded it.

Finally, he said, "I don't know exactly what I was thinking. I planned to go out, to avoid Tenny—she wasn't hurt was she?" He opened his eyes, looking for a response.

Tom shook his head and left the room. Maybe to check on Tenny.

Drew remembered her grabbing him, how he had pushed his way outside, shaking her hands off, or trying to. They'd just disappeared as he was fully in the snow, potentially infected.

"She seems okay," Amber said. "I'll check her shortly just

to be sure, though Minnett says Boyd is certain she didn't go outside."

"Could you have been influenced to go out there?" Amber asked.

"Once I was out, I realized what I was doing," Drew said. "I mean, I knew it all along but it felt noble. I had planned to go to the portal, hoping to toss myself through but it was too cold and I wasn't wearing a coat or anything. But as soon as I was out there, I realized how stupid the plan was."

Amber nodded. "It sounds like you might have been influenced."

"If the frost witches really wanted me dead, don't you think they could have done that by now?" Drew asked, puzzled.

Minnett jumped back up on the table from where she'd been resting on the counter.

Just as her feet touched the table, her head jerked up, like someone listening to something.

Drew felt it, too. Something had happened.

Amber hurried to the door but Minnett stayed on the table with Drew.

Without thinking, Drew grabbed the cat. Her fur was soft and warm beneath his fingers. Heat emanated from inside her and his fingers were so cold. He dug them in deeper.

Minnett gasped, the last of her air leaving her lungs.

Drew knew he ought to stop, but his fingers locked into her soft warm flesh, squeezing every bit of the warmth from the small body.

Amber turned from the door as soon Minnett squealed. The cat didn't make a sound out loud but Amber heard it in their telepathic bond.

Drew was sitting up, holding Minnett by the middle. His knuckles were turning white as he squeezed. Minnett's mouth was open, showing her little pink tongue. She was no longer purring.

Amber rushed Drew, pushing him towards the heat lamp. Better Minnett get a burn than die at his hands.

Drew let go of Minnett to stay upright on the table.

Minnett flew to the floor, hissing. It took only a moment for her to catch her breath. Amber wanted to kneel and examine her, but Drew was dangerous.

"So is Chase," Minnett thought. *"He has already harmed Stuart and Anson."*

Amber heard someone moving outside the door, probably going up the stairs. Drew stared at her. The being looking at her out of Drew's eyes held none of Drew's kindness or compassion.

Minnett started to grow. She passed the size of a bobcat

and kept on going. Amber hadn't seen her do that. She knew it was a power the guardian cats had, but didn't realize Minnett could do it.

"I have all their powers but do not typically need them," Minnett said. *"It is important in case I have to heal them psychically."*

Drew turned to the cat, ignoring Amber. Amber put up a shielding spell around herself to keep out any psychic influences and to make it harder for Drew to attack her. She wanted to put one around Minnett, but the cat was getting ready to fight.

"I can't heal anyone without you," Amber said. Not out loud of course. She wouldn't give the thing inside Drew, because this clearly wasn't Drew, the satisfaction.

"I do not intend to die," Minnett said. She was now the size of a bear, though she still looked like a cat. Her formerly tiny white feet and pink jellybean toes were the size of Amber's hand. The claws that had always been sheathed unless doing a healing now sprung from toes the size of Amber's thigh and had more in common with a scimitar than Minnett's claws.

Drew slumped down.

"Drew?" Amber asked.

He shook his head. 'They did it again, didn't they?"

"Has that happened before?"

Minnett didn't change sizes. She remained large and ready to spring. Her sleek muscles normally hidden beneath her plush black and white fur were apparent along her shoulders and hips. If Drew made the wrong move, he'd be dead.

Minnett's tail twitched once.

"I don't think so. But there was just this blank between the time that you were talking to me and now," Drew said. "I can't remember anything. I mean, Minnett's fur felt so warm. I knew I should let go, and I wanted to, and then… It wasn't like when Courtney talks about her field of dying flowers. I just wasn't anywhere."

"It is possible that he died outside and the frost witches brought him back just for such a use. I am not certain why one backed down now," Minnett said.

Thumps and crashes came from upstairs. Amber looked up at the ceiling. Minnett's ears flattened against her head, not because they nearly touched the ceiling, but because of what she was hearing.

"The thing in Chase is fighting the clowder," Minnett said, quietly. *"There will be injuries."*

Amber moved the heat lamp and pushed Drew back down. She considered putting restraints on him but remembered how easily Chase had broken through them. Heck, he'd apparently broken through the chain on his leg if he was upstairs.

"Can I go next door to check on Stuart and Anson?" Amber asked, looking at the cat.

"I can watch this one," Minnett said. Amber felt Minnett's sense of glee at the thought of taking Drew out, and that was most unlike the little healer cat she'd always known.

"Prey," was the only explanation Minnett gave. The image of normal cats hunting came to Amber and she realized that in this form, all of her hunter instincts were focused on Drew. Amber hoped that when she came back both Minnett and Drew were still alive.

COURTNEY

Snow splattered against the white mounds at Courtney's feet. She had stepped back so she was behind Grey. The shield he'd created to keep the frost witches from harming him impressed her the way an artist's rendering of the ocean would impress her with the colors and the brush strokes all working together to create a certain look.

Courtney added her strength to the shield behind which she now stood.

One of the frost witches disappeared. One moment there were three ice figures and the next two. Not even a wink or a glow. Courtney smelled no magic from them.

Dawn let her know that the frost witches could manifest something, change something, with a single thought. They just had to imagine what could be in this particular world.

Courtney wanted the frost witches broken. She closed her eyes, thinking about the witches being broken. Dawn guided the power. Breaking the ice figures would scatter them. Easier than trying to destroy them.

Courtney felt the old life energy of the trees, the more

delicate energy of the smaller bushes, the tiniest sparks from the insects deep in the earth. Dawn drew from the earth itself, the rocks and dirt that held memories of what had once been. That energy was solid.

Courtney absorbed the snow energy as it fell, bringing down the energy from the earth's outer atmosphere. Courtney imagined herself up there, absorbing energy before the light reached the clouds and caused the snow to fall. She separated the warmth and then the dampness and clouds formed, thicker and thicker above the city and spread over a wider area.

The power was intoxicating.

Dawn understood. More than understood. She'd lived that intoxication for her entire existence. Only in age had she become careless enough to wallow in it, and that was when it had been determined she needed to be destroyed.

The idea that Grey would feel the same intoxication niggled at Courtney. She couldn't think about that now. She had to focus.

Energy gathered, Courtney turned her attention to the ice figures, both of them. She focused on them the way she'd focused on her body when she was trapped in the field of dying flowers. She studied their hands, examined everything about them, her enhanced sight picking up information her human eyes could never have understood. After taking in the entire figure, knowing it as well as her own, she turned her attention to visualizing the figures exploding outward, shards flying, bouncing off the shields that Grey had set up.

Ice cracking and breaking shook Courtney. She hadn't quite believed what she was seeing until the noise reached her. No screams. Nothing.

The snow where the figures had stood became littered with slivers of ice. Almost immediately, one more figure stood before them.

It held out a hand and ice blasted at the shield. Courtney felt the cold. Small shards began to break through the thick shielding Grey had created and she'd strengthened. Grey struggled to keep the shield in place. Courtney focused on the figure, hoping it, too would shatter.

A long thing shard of ice hit the side of her face, drawing blood. The warmth spread down her cheek and dripped onto her shoulder.

The cold ate so deeply into Courtney that she didn't feel the pain.

She focused even harder on breaking down the figure. Nothing happened.

They learned.

Dawn suggested that she think smaller. More focus on one area to break concentration.

Courtney focused on hands. Hands were easier for her. She'd started there with her body. She focused on the hand breaking apart.

The cracking sound of ice was quieter. Only the hand disappeared, but for the moment the attack on them stopped.

Courtney imagined a drill hitting the figure. She knew her dad's tools well. He used them often in the house he'd persuaded her to purchase. She knew the shape of the drill, felt the smooth metal and weight of it as she handed it to him. The sides might feel warm if he'd just been using it, cool if not.

The smell of wood and heat reached her nose.

Courtney's imaginary drill, the size of an elephant appeared before them and started whirring its way towards the figure. No sound came from the drill but when it hit the ice, Courtney heard a high-pitched shriek that echoed through her bones.

Ice shattered, shards flying towards them. The shields

were permeable enough that Courtney was hit with flying ice.

Grey grunted once when fragments hit him.

Courtney let the image of the drill disappear.

"Are you okay?" she asked.

Grey raised his head. "As I can be. Interesting choices. I assume your witch has guided you?"

"She did," Courtney said.

"They aren't gone," Grey cautioned.

"No, but they've taken a blow."

"They'll return and hit us harder," Grey said.

"We can pick the place this time." Courtney was thinking about the clowder house. They'd have people to back them up, help them. She could add the power she could draw to that of the cats. Both cats and humans would have more than they ever had before.

"The clowder is under attack," Grey said.

Courtney checked in with Dawn who confirmed. Dawn wasn't as connected to the clowder house as Grey was. The cats had been created after she was supposed to have been destroyed. Her essence didn't infuse them so she knew less than he did, or that's how Courtney understood the explanation.

Dawn seemed uncomfortable that Grey would know things before she did. She was, however, impressed with what magical powerhouses the cats were.

Courtney turned to hurry through the thickly falling snow towards the clowder house. She had no fear of being infected.

"Can you be harmed by the snow?" Courtney asked.

"I cannot be influenced the way humans are," Grey said. "And they have not tried to possess me exactly. I believe that's what the original plan was. They hoped to harness my power that way. Unfortunately, you were more resourceful than they expected."

Courtney let the pull of the clowder draw her. She could barely see further than the length of her arm. Grey was only a shadow next to her, but she knew it was him.

He seemed smaller than he had been. Dawn whispered the word energy to her.

The single word spoke volumes in Courtney's mind. She understood the effort of appearing a certain way, a way that wasn't naturally part of the species. While they were shapeshifters and had no true look, certain ways of being were more natural than others. Human shapes were unnatural. Even the shield that he had around himself to keep the snow from hitting him took more energy than he could afford to expend.

Grey needed more energy, but he couldn't pull that much from the world without potentially damaging it. Courtney understood the world, the earth itself, was more important to the people of Cat Home than the humans that lived there. They understood things in a timeframe that was still beyond Courtney's understanding. It was like her trying to understand and empathize with a flea.

The ideas made Courtney want to drink in the energy of all humanity and destroy them. She knew they were bad for the environment. She ought to take all their lives.

Even as thoughts of destruction crossed Courtney's mind and a feeling of glee that infused her, she was hit with an image of her sister, Payton. Then she saw her friend, Hannah. They were both laughing by the lake where Courtney had met Chase.

She couldn't destroy all her friends and loved ones. Shame hit Courtney deep down in her gut.

"There is no shame in enjoying your newfound power," Grey said quietly. "You have yet to act on it. At the point you do, you will be destroyed like all the other witches we let out into the universe."

Courtney wanted to snap that he wasn't nearly as powerful as she was. Not on earth. On Cat Home, it might be different, but here the shape and body Grey had to assume and the fact that shifting didn't come naturally in this world kept him from his full power. Even on Cat Home, Dawn's more ancient knowledge and clear ruthlessness might allow Courtney to prevail.

"Others are coming," Grey said, once again reading her mind. "And we will never stop watching you."

Courtney shivered at the thought.

STUART

Small particles embedded themselves in Stuart's flesh. The icy cold from inside them broke apart and invaded the depths of his body. He felt every muscle and bone, every cell, freezing upon impact until he couldn't move, could barely think.

His eyes were open and he watched Chase stride past him. Watched the empty room in front of him.

"*We are ready,*" Trag's voice reached him. It felt distant. The words fuzzed with static.

Stuart didn't understand exactly what Trag and the other bond-mate cats were ready for. The most logical explanation was Chase, though Stuart didn't know what secrets the cats might have in order to be ready for him.

The ice made it hard to breathe. His chest still moved but it felt like heaving his way through a snowdrift, pushing and pushing only to take in the smallest amount of air, barely enough to keep him going.

His magic felt as sluggish as his mind. Even his heart beat more slowly than normal. He'd had a shield up and it had been nothing to the frost witch. While his abilities were nothing compared to Grey or Courtney, if Chase could do things like this so easily, Stuart despaired of ever being able to defeat the frost witches.

Amber walked in front of him. She reached out a hand to touch him. Stuart wanted to warn her about the ice. His mouth didn't move. The ice had frozen him solid.

He felt warmth where her hand touched him. She whispered something to him, but he couldn't hear. Stuart longed to ask her to repeat herself, to speak up, but couldn't form the words.

Ice creaked around him. He thought perhaps his fingers could move. They tingled and burned now that they weren't completely encased in ice.

His first thought was frostbite and wondered how to heal that. The burning increased. His arms ached.

He heard ice cracking and falling to the floor, but he didn't feel anything different. Stuart remembered that Anson had been in the room with him. He'd have been further from Chase's blast.

The thunk that sounded behind him suggested Anson had fallen down. The ice would have zapped their energy, feeding the creature in Chase. They were both left alive so they could continue to feed the frost witches. Stuart was certain of it.

He reached out to Trag. The cat didn't respond. Stuart got a sense Trag was busy.

As his ears thawed, he heard sounds from upstairs, heavy jumping and thumping. Even a short scream.

Stuart needed to be up there. He tried to move his legs, but nothing happened. Still stuck to the ground, he tried to draw magic.

The earth beneath the house offered him no power. No matter how deeply he sent his consciousness, he found nothing to draw from. A few insects, but he'd been taught to attempt to avoid drawing power from living creatures.

Like the frost witches, Stuart had been drawing life force. He just hadn't known it. The whole concept made him feel slimy. Normally, a bit of life force from an insect would have been buried beneath the greater force from the earth, the rotting and changing and heat from the center would all have given him force. A few insects caught up in his draw were nothing. Now there were only those few insects who had slipped through the force Chase and others had drawn.

Stuart reached outward towards other homes and the lake. The earth was barely hanging on. He had no idea how one revitalized dirt when the energy that made it living had been exhausted.

He was loathe to draw more from such a depleted area no matter what needed to be done.

Behind him, Anson grunted. The door squeaked as it opened. Stuart tensed against who might be there.

Amber appeared in front of him with a blanket, which she wrapped around his shoulders. The blue fleece fell to mid-calf and although he normally would have huddled happily beneath it, this time the blanket did little to warm him. Stuart thought longingly of summer days when he'd been a teen in Miami.

Being outside, sweating in the hot, moist air where you couldn't be cold no matter how hard you tried would be heaven about then. Though he hated the colder weather around Base Command, he'd never missed the sun the way he did at that moment. In Miami, this ice would unfreeze in minutes.

Deep down, he knew that the frost witches would get to even the sunniest places. They probably saved the warmest areas for last, to savor the life force, the brilliant huge insects and reptiles that would make for the best siphoning.

The noises upstairs abruptly stopped.

Stuart craned his neck to look at the ceiling wondering

what happened. Although his neck and head felt cold and damp, he was able to move. Breathing was easier.

He took a step. His leg lifted and moved, but it didn't hold his weight. He put his arms out to catch his fall.

His chest took the brunt of the fall onto the cold concrete floor. He expelled the air in his lungs with a deep grunt.

Stuart needed to get up and move. Something had happened.

"*Chase is now Chase again,*" Trag said. "*His frost witch left, at least for now.*"

"*Is anyone hurt?*" Stuart thought.

"*Minnett will have bruises from Drew. Shahanna is nursing a wound on her leg. Boyd has a deep scratch on his side. We expect that Amber will have no trouble healing us,*" Trag said.

"*I heard fighting on the first floor. I thought you were in the library?*" Stuart figured the witches had tried to divide and conquer. Taking Courtney and Grey from the house, then isolating him from the clowder was a good start.

"*We went into fighting stance,*" Trag said. "*All of us. Grey's proximity made the size change easier to hold. Minnett is still larger.*"

Trag sounded impressed. Depending upon when she'd taken on the larger size, it was an amazing feat. The cats could normally only hold the increased size for a short time. How long depended upon the cat, their human, and how large they became. Stuart was under the impression that the cats grew very large.

Amber came back.

"How are you?" she asked.

"Weak," Stuart mumbled. His voice came out softer than he intended.

His body burned and tingled. He wanted to close his eyes and sleep. He needed to get his wet clothes off and get warm. He needed food.

"Lean on me and see if you can get up. I'll move you to the medic room. There's plenty of heat in there," Amber said. "And I think I need to move Drew out of there and into here with Chase."

Stuart tried to look interested but wasn't sure he had the energy. Still, Amber relayed what had happened. That explained why Minnett had gone to fighting stance.

"Trag says several of the cats have wounds," Stuart croaked. He really needed fluids. Preferably warm.

"I know," Amber said shortly.

She managed to help him drag himself to his feet. Stuart did his best to help her move him but he couldn't really feel his feet and they tended to drag on the ground. Getting over the low doorstep took three tries before he got both feet over it.

Amber was starting to sweat, or perhaps he was dripping on her.

"Leave me sitting up here," Stuart said once they were in the hallway. "Maybe get me a fresh blanket and I'll start pulling off these clothing before they soak through. Hot tea with honey would be nice as well."

"Tom is making up hot cereal and tea. He'll be down in a few," Amber said. "I'll go find that blanket."

Stuart watched her go as he worked to pull off his flannel shirt. She'd clearly been struggling with keeping him up, otherwise, she wouldn't have let him sit in the hallway. He got the shirt off, but his head dipped down against his chest before Amber returned with a blanket.

CHASE

When the frost witch jumped into his body, Chase wasn't sent to his lake. Despite that, he couldn't make his body do anything. He couldn't stop his hand from raising, couldn't stop the ice from freezing Stuart and Anson. He couldn't help them as he walked through the room to get to the people upstairs.

Chase knew that one of the other frost witches had taken over Drew. He knew Minnett had been injured, but not how badly. The pleased feeling from the frost witch made his stomach turn in disgust. That, too, pleased the frost witch as it ate his emotions, feeding on the energy Chase's distress provided.

Upstairs, Tenny, Tom, Fin, Cari, Julia, and Matt waited for him. Chase's arm reached up to send ice into them, freezing them in place. His stomach turned at the need to devour at least one of them until there wasn't any life left.

Instead, something jumped at his back, something large.

He'd gone down, realizing it was one of the cats, having increased its size. Chase turned, or rather the frost witch did, and sent a jolt of energy through the cat, knocking it back against the wall.

Before he could raise his hand again, Chase was pressed down by Tom and Matt, the two largest of the men upstairs. Chase fended them off easily. The women rushed him. Fin came at him with his bo stick. The frost witch used ice to freeze Fin in place. At almost the same moment, it used energy to knock someone else off of them.

To have a frozen body on top of him would have held him down too quickly.

The cats all came downstairs. They weren't purring to make him sleep or to drop a net around him. They'd learned that those spells couldn't help. Instead, they were fighting. Claws were out, long thin nails that drew blood from Chase's arms and sides, and once, even his face.

He felt the sting while the frost witch kept fighting, twisting his body in ways a human wasn't meant to twist and using up energy Chase didn't think he had to spare. His joints ached with fatigue and the warm blood leaked down the side of his face and his arms. Chase worried that the frost witch would finally let him die in the fight.

Then just as suddenly as the witch had dropped into his body, it leaped out again.

Chase had been on his knees by that time. He fell face-down against the floor, barely turning his head to the side to keep from breaking his nose.

He closed his eyes, hoping to pass out. Naturally, that didn't happen. If the frost witch could have caused him more pain by letting him pass out, no doubt it would have.

The only saving grace was that the cats seemed to know the witch was gone.

"Riley says that Anastasia felt the witch travel out," Cari said.

Chase wanted to nod at her, agree, or perhaps even say yes, but nothing worked. His body weighed several tons. He didn't quite have the power to move his arms.

"Can you move?" Tom asked, crouching down near Chase.

Chase blinked. Worked on moving his fingers. He half-curled them into a fist.

"We have wounded cats. Stuart and Anson are also hurt," Julia said. "He can wait."

She gave him a look that said she might have been sorry. Maybe Chase was imagining that look. Maybe she wasn't sorry at all. He couldn't say that he would be.

His stomach growled.

Food would help. Fin brought him a glass of orange juice with a straw. Chase was able to sip from that. A few minutes later when the sugar hit his bloodstream, he was able to lift his head and move his arms to a more comfortable position.

He couldn't sit up on his own, but Tenny helped him, her strong, wiry arms practically lifting him off the ground. One he was sitting, Chase scooted himself so his back was against the sofa. He faced the kitchen where the others were making food.

The smells of melting cheese on quesadillas and grilled cheese sandwiches reached him. Tomato soup bubbled on another burner. Someone heated up something spicy smelling. Chase's stomach growled.

No one noticed. They were all busy eating and drinking. He longed for a soda or even more orange juice. He couldn't stand up and get it. Turning his head, he saw Trag, still over-sized, but not huge, watching him the way he might have once watched a mouse. If Trag thought Chase was possessed again the cat wouldn't hesitate to pounce, probably gaining size the moment his muscles tensed for the jump.

Chase was ready to chew off his own arm when Matt brought over some tomato soup and a can of soda. Things that were easy to swallow, although with the smells coming from the kitchen, Chase wanted to go over and eat three or four of the grilled cheese sandwiches and then maybe make several more sandwiches with whatever meat was in the refrigerator.

He chugged the soup and set the mug aside. Then he drank half a can of the soda. He'd have chugged the whole thing but who knew when they'd get around to feeding him more.

Cans of cat food were opened. Someone got out tuna and the cats got a treat.

Chase considered crawling over to the cat food dishes but even as the thought crossed his mind, Mack glanced up at him and glared.

"I couldn't do anything," Chase whispered.

No one looked at him when he said it. Trag glanced at him, but then went back to eating while Shahanna watched over him.

If only there were a way to keep the frost witches out of his body.

"*There is,*" someone whispered to him, telepathically.

Chase listened.

"*Die. Throw your life away. We'll eat your despair and the end of your life,*" the voice told him.

Chase closed his eyes. He didn't want to die. He noticed the wound on Boyd's side still leaking blood. Chase imagined how Tenny would feel if Boyd had died or been seriously wounded. Then he tried to imagine what she'd do to him if he were sitting there and she was suddenly catless. Bad enough that his frost witch had killed Drew.

At least Courtney had been able to bring Drew back. She wasn't around to save one of the cats. Chase wasn't sure if he could live with himself if he let one of the cats die because he couldn't manage his frost witch.

Maybe he did need to give up and die. He needed to do it in a way that kept the frost witches from being able to feed on his dying energy, though.

DREW

Drew watched Minnett. Her tail twitched now and then. Though she sat on the floor, her head reached higher than his own and she looked down on him with her great golden eyes.

The cats didn't assume their large forms unless they had to fight. Even then, they preferred to use the magic of their purrs to create shields and put the opponent to sleep. This emergency had required changing size. Drew didn't even feel the purrs from upstairs.

Instead, he heard thumps and bumps and once a growl. It sent chills down his spine. The blank time in his memories haunted him. The last he remembered was trying to get to the warmth deep inside the cat.

"How badly did I hurt you?" Drew asked Minnett.

She blinked at him. Kept her eyes narrow. Without Mack to tell him, it was as close as Drew could come to communication.

Guilt ate at him. He should have died outside. They should have left him.

"They should have left me outside," Drew said.

Minnett didn't blink. She just watched him.

Amber came through the door, practically dragging Anson. Drew dropped to the floor from the table.

Minnett growled, low in her throat. It might have been the furnace running but Drew knew better.

"Just helping. She needs it," he said.

He put his shoulder under Anson's arm.

"Thanks," Amber said quickly. "Third table. I need to help Stuart."

Drew helped Anson to the table.

"What happened?" Drew asked.

"Chase," Anson said. He spit the name out, not as if he were angry but more like he was so breathless he could hardly speak. Drew pulled the blanket that had covered him off the table and tossed it over Anson.

Doing so, Drew realized he was walking around in his underwear, the white fabric still damp and sticky around his lower body. His face flamed.

He went to the cupboard and found a heavy sheet to wrap himself in. Minnett kept a close eye on him. Of course, at her size, she kept a close eye on everyone.

She put a huge paw on Anson's belly. Claws extended. They looked as thick as sewing needles. Drew winced. Anson didn't seem to notice.

The cat half closed her eyes.

No doubt she was healing Anson, checking him over. Drew wondered if she was less vulnerable as a large cat than she was as a small cat. If something entered Anson and attacked her, would it be as painful?

He hated the part of him that wanted to experiment. Courtney had talked about the feeling of wanting to hurt people, the stray thoughts that made her want to scream because they were so out of character.

At least Courtney had been aware of when the witch took

over. She went to that field she talked about. Drew had noth-ing. Maybe he was still partly dead, a weird undead creature.

Minnett pulled her paw back. Drew saw it from the corner of his eye. The claws were still out. She held it up, looking at Drew. It might have been his imagination but he thought he saw her muscles tensing to swat him.

He didn't know if he'd care if she did. He'd hurt her.

Amber came back and got blankets. She didn't say a word.

Drew hopped back up on the nearest table, the one he'd been lying on. Dampness from the bottom sheet leached up into his butt, reminding him he was cold. The medic room had the heat on high, probably because he'd been hypothermic coming in.

Suddenly, he started to shiver. Drew hung his head, pulling the sheet more tightly around him. The heat lamp was out of reach but he didn't move to pull it over. He didn't deserve comfort. Not after what he must have done.

They should have let him stay dead. He had to find a way to die once more. Not some stupid stunt like walking outside and thinking of throwing himself through a portal. He needed a real plan.

The garage remained open when Courtney and Grey reached the clowder house. Though the gray clouds kept her from seeing it clearly, Courtney knew the door remained like a dark maw, ready to swallow her. Except that maw represented safety for her and Grey.

She reached out to Dawn, wondering if that was a thought Dawn had had. But the idea didn't come from her. It came from outside both of them.

Influence could be used against even other frost witches, the stronger influencing the weaker. Courtney and Dawn weren't as strong as the other four. They were alone. One on one, she and Dawn had the advantage of this being Courtney's home world. She and Dawn weren't strong enough to take on four.

The witches learned so quickly. Once, she could knock one down and shatter it. The next leap and they could withstand her pushing against them, standing not like ice sculptures but brick walls.

Expending the energy against the witches and keeping

herself warm made Courtney ache with hunger, both for food and life force. She let Dawn search around for the neighbors, looking for a group that hadn't already been siphoned. Everyone around had energy so low, it made Courtney and even Dawn hesitate to sip more.

"They're taking energy from the people around us," Courtney whispered, walking up the drive.

Grey didn't turn. "Of course they are. It is what they do. Leaving them alive as they have is smart. They can milk this world for a century if it's just the four of them."

"There were more out there at one time. Do you think four is all that's left?" Courtney didn't count Dawn. Dawn was part of her now. Together they were neither frost witch nor human.

"Some probably ended up like the one inside you, inadvertently meshing with a native species. Others would have been absorbed by the others, too weak to continue so their very life was consumed. We don't necessarily get more powerful as we age, but all of the witches feel very powerful, stronger than I am, and not because they've freely drawn energy in a way I cannot allow myself," Grey said.

Deep down Courtney knew there were more. Dawn's information flowed through her, letting her know the history, the fighting, who had been absorbed, and who had just been lost. The witches hadn't all stayed together. They traveled in smaller packs, the weaker witches avoiding those that had become more powerful. When it couldn't be avoided, they were often at the mercy of the most powerful. All of them avoided certain places, where there was something they didn't want to face. Courtney wondered what it was but Dawn avoided letting her see those thoughts and memories.

Dawn had been strong enough to exist with the strong

group. She'd come through the barrier first, influencing Chase and then finding a home in Courtney, like a seed planted, growing as she absorbed her emotions. Another had come through to find Chase and use him without him even noticing, thanks to Dawn's deep influence.

Courtney's abilities, the ability to cage Dawn, had sent alarms through other witches who still fed on the last planet. They came through the portals. They didn't need to use them exactly the way other species did. They could siphon energy from the portals or feed them to make the worlds turn and touch as they needed, though changing the paths of worlds was difficult. Carved movements set for the ages did not easily change and the paths went back to normal once the witches stopped working with them.

The garage felt warm after the outside. Courtney shook the snow from her head, but not before absorbing any energy left in the little flakes. That caused melting and only water flew from her hair.

Grey didn't take off his coat. He looked better, almost the size he'd been when Courtney had met him.

Courtney led the way between the cars. The door to the main house wasn't locked. She opened it. The warmth flowed out and around her. Dawn started drinking greedily from the heat. It felt good against the ache in Courtney's stomach but she couldn't take all of the warmth. The furnace wouldn't keep up.

Grilled cheese, tuna, and a variety of soup smells reached her. Courtney groaned just a little. Inside, Cari and Julia were still cooking. Tenny and Matt were wolfing down a variety of sandwiches, which rested on a small plate.

"What happened?" Matt asked, his mouth still full from a very large bite of grilled cheese.

Grey was already reaching for a sandwich, not saying a

word. Courtney grabbed another. Hers was tuna. She'd have preferred grilled cheese, but she didn't really care. Cari was already fixing another one while snacking on a snickers bar.

"The frost witches took us to the portal," Courtney said.

"The cats told us," Tenny replied, between bites. She might have more to say, but food took precedence.

"I think we beat back three of the frost witches. One got back to Chase and then it returned to our fight. I think after that it fled into Chase's body again," Courtney said.

The other four looked at each other.

Courtney glanced back. Chase was on the floor, apparently asleep. A hand twitched. An empty glass sat next to him.

"We made sure we perked his energy up but didn't want to give him too much," Julia said. She glanced at Grey.

Grey's sandwich was gone.

"It will just feed on any life force around. Everyone around this area has appallingly low energy, even the land. They've been overfeeding with all the battles," Grey said. "I can search out energy from further afield."

Courtney let Dawn search out some energy from further away. It was harder for her. Grey was less connected to his form. Still, Dawn was able to reach outside the general area and draw energy. The land she pulled from was slightly depleted. Someone had reached it before she had, but there was enough to take without destroying it.

Courtney felt better. She went to the pantry to find something else to eat. She needed something warm. She opened a can of chili and put that in a bowl to heat in the microwave. It wasn't her favorite thing, but it would be hot and the spices would warm her insides further.

Cari pulled out a huge pot of water to heat. They'd make pasta. Julia or Tenny would start making spaghetti sauce, with meat. They'd all need the carbohydrates.

Courtney searched for Tom but ran into the energies from the bond-mate cats. Their energies were larger than normal. The magic around them sparkled with power. She had to restrain Dawn from pulling energy from them. Once reminded, Dawn was okay not siphoning.

After passing through the feline energy, even one very large amount of energy that belonged all to one cat, Minnett, Courtney realized, she found Stuart. His energy was appallingly low.

"What happened to Stuart?" Courtney asked.

"Chase," Matt said. He grabbed another grilled cheese the moment Julia flipped it out onto a plate.

The bell on the microwave dinged and Courtney pulled out her chili. She stirred and tested and put it back in for a bit longer. It didn't stop her from taking one quick bite of the barely warm food.

"He sent a blast of cold and Stuart and Anson were caught in it," Tenny said. "Boyd says Anson is resting in the medic room. Stuart is in the hallway because Amber couldn't move him any further. Tom went down to bring food and then help him up. Amber is working on Boyd."

Courtney noted a few traces of blood on the floor. Cat food dishes sat around, all empty. Normally they were fed upstairs now. The smell reached her. Riley fed the unwounded in her library.

No doubt Tom would bring more food down for the wounded cats and humans after he settled Stuart.

Grey opened the refrigerator. He grabbed a hunk of cheese and began gnawing on it, eyes practically closed.

Courtney wolfed down her chili when it finished heating. It burned the roof of her mouth but Dawn healed that, taking the heat of the energy and using it for her own purposes. Courtney was still hungry, but her stomach no longer ached.

Grey went to close the garage door. Courtney knew he

added some power to the shields out there, as well as adding a warning. She'd know when the frost witches returned.

The sofa called her. Courtney walked over and laid down, falling into a deep sleep the moment she touched the cushions.

Amber worked on Boyd. He'd been scratched deeply. He laid on his side on the second table, since Stuart still hadn't made it to the medic room. Boyd's beige and brown fur felt thick and slightly dry beneath her fingers. His skin moved easily, the soft pad of normal fat and muscle beneath it slightly warmer than it should be as healing set in. He watched her with deep blue eyes. Boyd was bigger and the brown on his muzzle, feet, and tail was darker than Fin's smaller Siamese, Chara. His eyes were even darker like the lake on a cloudy day. Chara's eyes were lighter, almost turquoise.

Amber appreciated the energy she felt in Boyd's body. She'd managed to heal him enough that the long scratch, really more like a cut, didn't bleed. She now picked up the cordless clippers and shaved carefully around the spot.

Minnett talked Boyd through exactly what Amber was doing, so although the clippers made a noise and the razor probably tickled against his skin, Boyd lay still. His eyes closed as she worked. Once she had shaved the area and created a clean field, Amber swabbed the wound and the area around it with tamed iodine.

Boyd flinched slightly at that and Amber paused. Normally it didn't hurt when she cleaned a wound. Boyd relaxed again.

"*Cold,*" Minnett said.

Now that Anson was getting warmer and Tom had brought food, Minnett was back to her normal size. She'd gotten fed the last time Tom had come down. Boyd was the last of the cats to get healed. While they were all definitely wounded—Amber didn't like the limp Wilbur had had but it wasn't as bad as she first thought—none of the wounds were as bad as they could have been.

"*We were lucky,*" Minnett said. "*Courtney and Grey kept them just off-balance enough that they couldn't quite coordinate attacks. They used Chase as an attack of opportunity when Courtney hit his frost witch. The same with Drew.*"

Amber used butterfly bandages on the cut. On a normal cat, they might not have worked as they were easy enough for a determined cat to peel off, but Boyd understood what she was doing. He'd probably have been fine without them but the cut was longer than she liked. She'd started the healing process and made sure no shadows from the frost witches had taken root inside him.

All the cats were clear.

Amber stood back when she was done. Boyd continued to lay there. He moved slowly, awkwardly, not liking the feel of the bandages. Amber didn't need Minnett to translate that.

Drew snored lightly on the table next to her. As soon as Anson thought he was ready to move, he and Tom would move Drew to Chase's room. Chase was still upstairs. Amber hated putting the two of them together, but she couldn't think of where else to hold Drew.

"*Back in his room,*" Minnett said. "*Courtney and Grey are good at warning shields and those take very little energy. We'd know the moment something changed. He'll feel better and it will keep the two of them apart."*

"*A lock would delay him more,*" Amber thought. "*Like on the door here. If Stuart and Anson hadn't been in there…*"

"*Anson might have died without Stuart's shielding,*" Minnett said. "*It may not have deflected much but it was enough to keep the two of them alive. Chase wasn't messing around when he threw that bolt. It would have taken him barely a second to destroy the door. It's probably lucky they were in the room.*"

Once again Amber felt frustrated and unsure. They had creatures that could punch through walls with barely a thought. Creatures that summoned ice and frost without any effort, just by feeding on the world around them. They manipulated people, including bond-mates. They infected people and sometimes she managed to heal those people, but not always. Amber's gaze lingered on Drew.

He looked normal. He was breathing evenly. The snore sounded normal. She moved over to the table to examine his physical energy fields. Amber placed her hand as lightly over his belly, above the blanket so as not to wake him.

She felt Minnett joining her. Minnett didn't jump to the table, but sat on Amber's foot, the physical connection allowing a closer and easier bonding. Together they examined Drew's organs.

His energetic physical body was paler than normal. Amber often saw the organs in the colors her medicine associated them with. The stomach and spleen were yellow, sometimes dark gold but in Drew's case, the yellow was closer to off-white. The liver and gallbladder would be green. Again, these were a greenish-gray, as if there wasn't even enough energy to show that there were problems.

The kidneys, which should have been black or dark blue, looked gray. Even the white of the lungs and the lower intestines was a foggy white like something had dirtied it. Not dark enough to be true shadows but murky. The heart area was light red, not pink so much as a red that had water washed through it.

Amber had already searched for shadows along Drew's spine and it remained clear. Perhaps it took a full day for his shadows to reappear. Normally, she always found shadows.

Next, Amber sank lower into his energetic field, looking at his psychic or spiritual energetic field. There, once again, she was met with nothing. Minnett poked at the nothing, but like hitting air, there was no real change.

Then, darkness rose, threatening to engulf them.

Amber mentally pulled Minnett with her as they hurried out of that plane and through Drew's physical body.

Shadows like snakes met them, curling and swirling around. One of the snakes struck at Minnett, its shadow mouth dangerously close to the cat's paw.

Amber had no idea what would have happened if it had connected.

Her breath caught. Amber's eyes flew open as she struggled to take in more air. She was back in her body.

Minnett had leaped across the room so she had space to grow.

Drew's hands grabbed at Amber's neck. He stared at her with eyes that looked half dead.

Someone, probably Anson, pulled at the hands, pulled at Amber, trying to get her away from him.

Amber felt something in her neck pop. She waited to fall to the floor dead, her neck snapped, but it was just the sound of a vertebra readjusting itself under the pressure.

Her lungs burned as she gasped for air that wouldn't come.

Her vision swam.

She thought Tom came in, but wasn't sure.

The hands disappeared from her neck and she lay on the floor, drawing in deep breaths. Her throat burned.

Amber scrambled back as Drew pulled himself up again, turning to face his new opponent.

Minnett leaped into the fray, swatting him with a paw the size of Amber's head. She watched, through clearing vision as Minnett opened Drew's cheek, blood spurting across the room in a red arc.

Amber's mind immediately examined the color, distressed by how pale and thin the blood looked.

Drew slumped over, the frost witch having attempted an attack, now fleeing once more.

Anson helped Amber up, though she felt his own unsteadiness as he reached down. Tom stood across the table from where Drew had rested, a pool cue in hand. Of course, the cues were still there, despite the lack of a table.

Drew's cheek bled and Amber noticed a darker area around his temple, probably where Tom had clubbed him.

She sighed. She'd need to work on healing him now. Amber started to move Drew into position on the table.

Tom put his hand over hers. "No. What if the frost witch is waiting for you and Minnett again? This is the second time it's attacked while you were examining him."

Amber knew Tom was right. It still hurt to leave one of her friends lying there, clearly in need of healing. Behind her, she heard Anson stumbling back to his bed.

Minnett shrank down to her normal size.

"I'm really quite hungry," she said.

The energy expended to change sizes twice in one day would be wearing on her. Amber had to get food. She was almost as tired as Minnett.

"Why don't you and Minnett lay down?" Tom said. "Tenny and Fin are on their way to help me move Drew out of here. When he wakes, we'll take him upstairs. We'll get Chase back in the basement room, okay?"

Amber nodded. She had to rest. Hopefully, while they did all that someone would bring her and Minnett food. Anson would need more, too.

She drifted off as she thought about all the things that needed to be done.

S tuart's nose itched and tickled with the smell of magic. That scent of burnt candles recently snuffed swirled around him, eating back down through his nose and into his throat. It colored the flavor of the oatmeal and the grilled cheese Tom had brought down. Even the coffee tasted burnt.

Just as Stuart made his first attempt to stand, his arms pushing his body upright, the smell got stronger than ever. More magic.

He felt it that time, the slight temperature decrease that was enough to start his body shivering. Whatever good the hot cereal had done him disappeared.

Stuart slumped back down in a pile. He heard Tom coming back down the stairs, practically running. No one else followed. Minnett growled again, the sound too loud for the little cat. Stuart knew she'd used magic.

The frost witches were active, then, still. He waited for sounds from upstairs, but nothing happened. Just some people walking around up there, but no thumps or irregular stomps suggesting that Chase had woken and started fighting them again.

Stuart needed to get back on his feet. Even Grey and Courtney together could use his help. His comparatively small amount of power might be what enabled them to tip the scales in their favor. With the world on the line, Stuart couldn't afford to be too tired to move.

He pushed himself back up. Leaving the mugs and the plate on the floor to be cleaned up later, he leaned against the wall and pushed himself towards the medic room. The heat lamps in there would help his body warm up. They would allow him to conserve what energy he had.

Fin reached the bottom of the stairs. Fin carried food. Stuart's mouth watered at the smells of bacon and egg from a breakfast sandwich. Even the open dish of cat food drew him, though he knew that was for Minnett. If Amber couldn't get upstairs to feed the cat or Minnett wasn't able to make it up there, they were really hurting.

"Minnett is fine," Trag said. *"Just hungry. As is Amber. Drew attacked Amber this time."*

Tenny hopped onto the bottom stair. She held another sandwich and several cans of soda.

"Heard you needed food too," she said.

Tenny moved her body so that Stuart could lean against her instead of leaning against the far wall to continue to the medic room. Her shoulders were thin but strong. She didn't wince as he put his weight on her shoulder, for which he was thankful.

"I'm starving, again," Stuart said. "I need to get my energy back. If the witches keep after us, harrying us…"

"Why don't they just out and out fight us?" Tenny asked. "They could destroy us. Practically did. It was only that they pulled Grey and Courtney away that allowed us to fight them off. The one in Chase had to go help the others. But now we're all together again. I'm not sure we're a match for them. All they have to do is think something and it happens. Why not just destroy us?"

"Energy," Stuart said. "They aren't stupid. They know that with our magic and our connections that we generate more energy than the average human. They aren't killing many other humans. The deaths that happen are out of anger and frustration, sometimes depression that was brought up in the storms. They feed on that. They like emotions. Letting us stew, scaring us. That has to be a feast. If they kill us, that energy source is gone. They will though, just like they're destroying the land under us. At some point, they have to to keep feeding. We don't regenerate enough to keep them happy. The lower our energy, the less we have to emote."

Tenny glanced over at him before turning slightly so that they could get through the medic room door together. Amber grabbed the sodas. Stuart noted the distinctive colors of the Dr. Pepper on the can she opened. The other was blue. Probably Pepsi. For him.

The sugar called him. His body ached for it. Easy energy.

Drew lay half on the first table and half off, as if he'd tried to get up but didn't quite make it. He was breathing. No one had helped him.

Tenny noticed his look. "Boyd said it was bad in here for a bit. He'd just walked out the door when the frost witch jumped into Drew and tried to kill Amber. He only held purr magic because of his wound."

Tenny sounded defensive as if Boyd was worried about being judged. Amber was chugging her soda as if she'd not been injured at all. The only sign of problems was the angle at which Drew lay on the table and the rate at which Amber and Minnett were eating.

Stuart sat on the second bed and ate the food Tenny brought him. More breakfast sandwiches. Then the soda.

Stuart closed his eyes, savoring the feeling of his belly getting what it craved.

He opened them to see Fin, Tom, and Tenny moving Drew out of the medic room.

"They're taking him upstairs to his room," Trag said to Stuart's not quite formulated query.

"Are they going to bring Chase down?" Stuart asked.

"Yes."

Drew and Chase were the people that would allow the frost witches in. One on the first floor, one in the basement. Apart but not as far as they'd tried to keep Courtney and Chase. For the moment, Stuart trusted her. Grey seemed to take her truce with Dawn at face value. Stuart wasn't quite as certain.

They only had to keep going until reinforcements arrived in a few hours. Less than a day. They needed a strategy. Grey would be the one who had the most knowledge but Stuart wasn't sure he'd be all that helpful. Grey was used to thinking about something and having it come to him.

That ability didn't lend itself to planning. Someone else had to plan. Courtney didn't know enough, although Dawn's presence would help. However, Dawn would behave more like Grey, without planning. There was no strategy. Opportunities presented themselves. Cats waiting at the mouse hole for the mouse to peek out.

The mice needed a plan.

CHASE

Chase pretended to be asleep. He couldn't take the way the others were looking at him. Besides, it felt good to let his eyelids droop. Fatigue actually did make his entire body feel heavy. Even if the clowder would trust him to take himself back to his basement prison room, he wasn't sure he'd make it without assistance.

His stomach growled and he was tempted to open his eyes and hope someone would feed him. However, he'd sat there before and no one had.

The lack of attention made him angry, sort of. He was so tired that the only emotion he could really work up was annoyance. Chase kept his face neutral. Such a poor emotional showing wouldn't feed any of the frost witches.

Courtney showing up and flopping down easily on the sofa irritated him, too. He was a little more able to work up a feeling about that. Still not enough emotion to warm him, to build his energy, to break free of whatever the frost witch had done to him.

Chase had always been able to sense the presence there, a sort of secondary voice in the back of his head suggesting things that disgusted him even as they tempted him. For the moment that voice was gone.

As he'd learned, the creature could jump into and out of him far too easily and too quickly. If Stuart and Courtney had a spell to warn them when the witch made the jump, they hadn't bothered to tell him. Maybe they weren't even protecting him, just the room.

Drew had tried to leave, to jump through the portal. Maybe he had the right idea.

Grey left the kitchen. Chase listened for the sounds of someone climbing the stairs but Grey didn't make that much noise. He moved silently. A bit like the frost witches.

Chase kept his breathing even. He wanted to cry when he heard Cari and Julia start cleaning up the kitchen. Even so, if they left, he could stand up and get something easy from the pantry. Anything that would make the ache in his belly go away.

Chase considered Drew's flight out the door. They'd brought him back in without a coat. Chase gathered that he'd practically frozen just behind a car in the driveway.

Without the frost witch, Chase couldn't count on staying warm, so he needed his heavy coat. He remembered his first walk out into the snow, how disorienting it was. He remembered being cut off from Trag and how panicked he'd been. Chase knew Trag had bonded with Stuart. His frost witch had fed on that energy. Then it had fed on the sorrow that Chase felt knowing Trag was willing to move on.

Chase could get a coat if he could get himself to move. If he had more energy, he might have enough of the witch's power left to slip away. For that, he'd need more food. He didn't know how to pull energy from other people.

He knew how to set the portal to take him to a dead space between worlds. It wouldn't be just a dead area where a world had once lived. It would be a true dead space. Chase had seen that in the consciousness of the frost witch once, back before it had taken over and sent him to his lake. As much as he'd like to spend more time on that lake, without a care in the world, the witch had left him.

Even if it hadn't left him, it was his duty to Trag and to the people who had once been his friends to destroy himself. No matter what changed, Chase would always be vulnerable to the frost witches and perhaps even other symbiotic creatures.

He pushed himself up.

Cari tensed. Julia had a taser in her hand before Chase rose to his full height.

"Just hungry," Chase said. "Maybe cheese and crackers?" Surely that wouldn't be too much to ask.

The two women looked at each other again, trying to decide.

Courtney's soft snores stopped.

"It's not the witch asking. While Chase is less use to it now, the more energy he has, the more likely he'll be able to fight it," Courtney said.

Chase wondered how she'd heard them while she slept or if that was even Courtney talking.

He could have been like her, making peace with his frost witch, becoming one with it. Chase remembered the feel of the hunger, the craving. He shuddered. He wouldn't pay that price.

Julia put down the taser and went to the pantry and pulled out crackers. Cari pulled out some cheese. After a moment, she also pulled out a Coke for him.

Chase stumbled over, barely able to stand, and ate the crackers and cheese quickly, before guzzling the soda. The sugary liquid made it easier to think, though his limbs were still heavy.

When he finished, wondering if he could ask for more, Chase turned to see Courtney sitting up, looking at him.

"We know what you plan. I'm not sure you're wrong. I won't stop you if it seems like it will help, but for the moment, it won't," Courtney said.

There was something she wasn't saying, something he needed to understand. Chase wasn't sure what it was, just that from her expression, all Courtney, he knew she wanted to say more. How often had he cut her off about where to eat dinner and she'd had that look and then turned away for a few minutes, telling him she was getting ready, and returned with a smile?

There was more there.

By the time Tom and Fin came back up to help him downstairs, Chase realized Courtney wanted him to make sure he waited to go through the portal to that dead space until a frost witch inhabited him. Chase would need to make sure he had enough control to still set the portal and throw himself through.

Chase didn't think such a thing was possible, not for him. Courtney might have been able to do it, but he was going to need help.

Safe in his bedroom, Drew tried to sleep. He hurt all over. His eyelids didn't want to stay open, but even closed, lying on his side, sleep eluded him. It wasn't even that he was thinking too much. He'd lay there and stare at the darkness behind his eyes.

Sleep just wasn't coming. When the day had turned dark and night had fallen, Drew got up to try and read. Again, nothing. He had stashes of breakfast bars in his room and he ate one of them. His body craved something more filling but he feared opening the door to see one of the clowder judging his inability to control the frost witch that had jumped into him.

Drew knew they had to all hate him. He'd hurt a cat. He remembered his feeling of outrage when Chase had talked about hurting Trag, when Chase had tried and failed. Drew had actually hurt Minnett, not seriously, thankfully, but he'd felt the ribs crack as he'd squeezed.

Even now, in his room, without the frost witch, he heard that sound. He hadn't been there. He'd just been gone, perhaps dead once more, his body reanimated by a frost witch, but he heard the sounds of ribs cracking. He'd been told that he'd done that, though Minnett had been healed once she was larger.

Amber had added energy to her cat after the other cats had been healed. Apparently, they'd even had a purr circle. Drew had felt the energy swirling around him, had hoped that would relax him but it only agitated him.

So, he sat in his chair, not leaning back to relax, not picking up his Kindle to read, not doing anything. He stared at the off-white walls, the photos he had arranged of him and his family from happier times.

The memories were hard to hold onto. Drew tried to picture his mother's face as she'd worked in the kitchen. He remembered her jeans and her hair, braided down her back with a big black bow holding it in place. She smelled like lavender and spice and a slightly musky smell that grew stronger from time to time.

Drew remembered the firmness of her arms, the sharpness of her voice when she was angry, and the sounds of her singing when she was happy. He remembered the way she called him to her when she needed to drive him somewhere. He remembered the sigh of frustration when he brought home yet another stray.

He could not picture her face.

He remembered they had six cats at one point, mostly thanks to him. He couldn't remember what a single one of them looked like, only that one was black but didn't look quite like any of the solid black watcher cats.

If his return from the dead wasn't a first, Drew would have asked if losing your memories was normal. Maybe dementia happened because you weren't actually supposed to be there. His brain or wherever memories were stored—Amber said in the cells of the body—was still trying to shut down no matter that Courtney had poured life energy into him.

Drew needed to accept the fact that he was dead. He might keep walking around, talking to people, but the man he was had died. He'd had a month to get used to it. He'd read a lot of books, tried to reconnect with Kayley. Though they stayed close, the relationship didn't feel the same. Drew would have said Kayley acted differently towards him. Now, trying to remember his mother's face and the faces of the cats he'd had as a child, he realized he might be the one acting differently.

He had no idea if walking out into the snow was the first odd thing he'd done. Nothing else would have mobilized the clowder like it had. Drew thought he'd been used. He couldn't be sure he hadn't been used for other small things. Maybe he'd unlocked a hurricane shutter so that the neighbors could come in.

Maybe he'd made a bomb to blow up the house.

The last scared him. The only comfort Drew had was that he didn't have a clue about how to make an explosive. He'd never woken up with a strange substance on his fingers, nor had his bathroom smelled strange. Besides, the clowder kept a close eye on him, particularly Kayley.

Drew heard, or perhaps felt, the cats begin to purr again. This was a higher-pitched purr, faster moving. Energy then.

He could use the energy.

Closing his eyes, Drew leaned back in the chair. The energy swirled in the air, smelling faintly like a candle that had just been snuffed.

Mixed in with the candle smell was the scent he associated with ice. It felt cold. Drew shuddered thinking about it.

He tried to tell himself it was just Courtney adding her own energy to the spell, but he couldn't shake the sense that the witches were attempting to feed on this energy spell. If they'd been damaged enough to leave Drew's body just as he was killing Amber or Minnett, they must need the energy.

Drew felt it then, the tingle down his spine, the chill that invaded his chest. The frost witch was returning to his body.

Opening his eyes again, trying to sit up straight, Drew hoped to hold on to consciousness, but only lasted about two minutes.

With his last thoughts, Drew threw all his energy into sending a message to Mack. The frost witch was back inside him. Drew figured the message was hopeless but it was all he could do to attempt to warn the clowder.

They weren't going to have as much time as they hoped.

Courtney didn't rest as long as she would have liked. Her stomach growled and she got up and made more food. She practically pulled items at random from the refrigerator. Dawn searched for small pockets of life force that hadn't been too depleted. Both eating and the siphoning of energy made Courtney feel better.

When the bond-mate cats started purring, building energy, she let Dawn absorb the magic as needed. She was aware of Grey taking some of the energy. The clowder members, those who were actually human, as well as the cats, passively absorbed energy. Courtney felt as if she were in a crowd and Grey was the pushing person behind her, trying to force her to move.

Dawn noticed the frost witches in the house. First, the icy energy flowed around the house, checking on them. Dawn walled Courtney's thoughts away, made sure they didn't react to anything.

Then it flowed downstairs to Chase. The temperature in the house dropped and the furnace clicked on. The warm air moved Courtney's hair just a little. Her arms still had goose-bumps. Dawn hadn't felt it was the time to keep her warm.

Another draft blew through the house. It really did feel like the drafts that sometimes came up under the backdoor in the kitchen of Courtney's parent's home. Her dad had put in extra insulation and made sure all the doors and windows were sealed as well as possible but every now and then the wind would blow at just the right angle to create a draft beneath the backdoor.

This was like that. The draft faded nearly as quickly as it had come, though Dawn followed the energy back to Drew's room.

Two witches in the house. The cats had felt it too, or perhaps Grey and Stuart warned them because the purring stopped.

The house went still. Three frost witches plus the one who had been inside Chase. Two were there. That left two somewhere, waiting.

Courtney strained her ears against the hum of the furnace, the only thing that moved or made a sound. She tried to keep her breathing even. She smelled Kayley's scent from the living room. It was starting to change, to add the sweet and rotten aroma of fear.

Courtney wrinkled her nose. Drew's scent remained almost unchanged but for the faint traces of icy water.

Muscles tense, ready to move, Courtney waited. Inside her, Dawn was equally tense, waiting for whatever shields or magic needed to be thrown. Upstairs, someone walked down the hall. The slow movement suggested Riley.

Even with Dawn's enhancements, Courtney couldn't smell anything from that far away. She needed to know who was walking around. Everyone else was frozen except for Riley.

The heavy thump of Riley's walk echoed on the stairs.

Kayley drew in a breath loud enough to reach Courtney's ears.

The sound released Courtney to head to the stairwell.

Riley stood there, straighter than usual, her face blanker than usual. Normally Riley shifted a bit even standing still, all ways to keep her aching muscles from tightening up further. Now she acted like Grey.

Riley smiled. Not the way the normal Riley smiled but more like Grey smiled. A gesture that wasn't exactly that.

"We have taken an idea from the frost witches. The researcher agreed to this temporary housing so we would have another person here to fight with you," Riley said.

Kayley's eyes got big and she moved back.

Riley didn't smell like ice. She smelled faintly of feline musk and something Courtney associated with Stuart.

"Do you have all your powers?" Courtney asked.

Two other sets of feet hurried down the stairs. Probably the third floor. Grey and Stuart.

"Like the witches, we are constrained but not terribly. Others are coming. This type of possession is not without risks. The researcher consented to such risks," Riley said.

Grey appeared behind Riley. He looked her over, only his eyes moving to take her in.

Stuart stood on the step behind him. He stood taller, moved easier than he had earlier, but Courtney felt a sort of emptiness about him. He needed more energy. Without being able to feed on the energy of life force and emotion, it would take him much longer to regain his strength.

"Why doesn't Base Command lend people? They aren't that far away," Courtney said.

Grey and Riley turned to stare at her. The emptiness behind the eyes bothered her. Or maybe it wasn't emptiness exactly but a lack of reaction.

"Base Command has a hard time coming out in public,"

Stuart said. "They are like me, both human and not. Those who look human enough not to get stopped, like me, have little power compared to the frost witches. The command cats are sending what energy they can through links to me and to the other bond-mate cats. For someone to possess them, it would still take hours to get here."

Courtney didn't want to contemplate that not all the workers at Base Command looked human. Dawn silently chuckled in her mind, thinking about the restrictions of the laws of this world and shape changers. When cells get the ability to change, they want to, but it wasn't something they could control. Often they took on shapes from their imaginations and dreams. Given that each of them had had a bond-mate cat at one time, Courtney had a feeling that many of them looked more like cats than like people.

She felt Dawn's amusement at the image of a large cat walking on hind legs in a dress.

Grey turned his head towards her as if he heard her thoughts. Courtney worried he had, unless Dawn had prevented it.

Something drove through the shields around the house. Courtney felt them ripping apart. Her ears popped and her chest hurt. Stuart doubled over.

Grey appeared unmoved, though he seemed less stable than he had before.

Something banged against the front of the house. It sounded like someone had driven a tanker trunk into the wall, except that the wall still stood. Shards of glass fell from the half-moon window in the door.

A piece of glass hit Riley's slippered foot, though the pointed part of the shard hadn't faced down. She looked down and then kicked it off to the floor where it landed with a small clink against the other pieces.

Icy air flowed in, so deep and cold that Courtney shivered

a bit before Dawn started warming her. Reflexively she put up a shield near the window, but that was broken through seconds later.

From down the hall, she heard the door open. Smelled Drew.

In the basement, a door slammed open.

The frost witches were coming.

STUART

Stuart stepped up the stairs to the second step up. He'd been planning to go up to his room, but the witches had arrived. His feet crushed the carpet. The icy cold didn't hit him quite so hard up there. Riley, Grey, and Courtney would all be able to draw energy to them to warm themselves. Stuart didn't have that advantage.

"Let them know I'll volunteer to host someone," Stuart thought to Trag. It couldn't be any more dangerous to him than it was to Riley.

"Your cells are neither human nor other at this point," Trag said. *"So they can't just jump into your body and take over. They have discussed possibly taking over Mack as he does not have a human but no one is certain how that would affect the magic and now is not the time to find out."*

The burnt candle smell of magic surrounded him. It was so strong Stuart might have been in a Cathedral lit only by candles. Power reached him. Not just energy, but focus. The cat's power had been boosted.

"Those that came through the portal in France have arrived and should be here in an hour or so. The one riding Riley expended

much energy to get here and is using up much of her life force to compensate. It thought it would have more time to replenish."

Its arrival was no doubt one reason the frost witches were attacking now. They knew that the clowder was still weak. Depending upon how far they had gone to source life force or how much emotion they had encountered, the witches were likely better off than the clowder was.

Stuart let the magic of the cats flow over him, allowing himself to absorb the energy. His muscles ached less. His head no longer hurt. He felt as if he could stand up for as long as necessary. He might not move as easily as he'd like but he could fight.

Amber came down and stood behind him. She added some personal shielding to everyone. Stuart felt the magic like a soft blanket. She'd probably cultivated that sensation in her treatment room. People would be wrapped up in real blankets but also in magical ones.

"Move to the side," Trag said.

Stuart and Amber moved as one, standing near the wall.

Grey took point in front of the door. Riley waited behind him. Kayley stayed in the living area, her body tensed and ready. Fin appeared behind her, along with Anson, Matt, and Julia.

Someone pounded on the lower stairs. Stuart knew it was Chase. Either one of the cats had called off whoever was supposed to be guarding the door down there or they were down.

"We felt Chase moments before. Matt and Anson hurried up here," Trag said.

From the sounds, Chase was in no hurry.

Drew walked down the hallway, equally slowly. The witch would have calculated that anticipation would create emotion that they could feed on.

Drawing in a deep breath, Stuart worked to calm himself.

He heard Drew and Chase stepping more heavily than normal. It made them sound bigger than they were. The cats might be able to change size. Grey could probably do it. But Chase and Drew couldn't do it. Whatever the frost witches needed to do, they either had to leave Chase and Drew's bodies or use what magic they could through those bodies.

"They're still far more powerful than we are," Trag said, in response to any limits on magic the witches might encounter in a human form.

They'd attempted to tranquilize Chase, which hadn't worked. They'd knocked him out, though, but only after Courtney had worn out that frost witch. Stuart was thinking back to that time, trying to come up with a plan to fight them when the door blew open.

He had been expecting it to come off its hinges but the door only slammed open, hitting the doorknob of the closet by the stairs when it flew back that far open.

Grey hadn't even raised a hand when Stuart felt the magic pour from him.

Riley worked easily with him.

Courtney had turned to meet Drew and Chase.

Stuart took a step down to go help Courtney when Mack leaped over him. The orange tabby had grown to the size of a tiger, a particularly large tiger. Stuart slammed into the wall.

One of the frost witches came through the door, an ice sculpture image of a human being. He knew from Courtney that's what she had met near the portal.

It had to be the easiest form for them to assume. Ice was their friend. Based in water there was a certain flexibility in that shape.

Frost grew on the ceiling. Amber ducked. Tom and Tenny started down the stairs next. Stuart hurried with them, throwing up what shields he could to protect Amber's shields. No doubt the frost witches could break them down easily enough but double shielding would handle more power.

Grey sent out an energetic blast that pushed one of the witches through the door. Riley used something like a red laser light to cut off the legs of the other.

While both things worked, the magic only worked for a second. Still, it was long enough for Tom, Tenny, and Stuart to get behind them, to battle either these witches or Drew and Chase.

Kayley was already battling with Drew while Courtney took on Chase. The two were circling each other.

Stuart reached for power, intending to try knocking Drew backward even as Tom and Tenny threw themselves at him in tandem. Both slammed into an invisible wall.

Stuart narrowed his eyes. Then he closed them, reaching out to unpick the details of the spell while Kayley kept Drew occupied.

He heard, rather than saw Tom and Tenny get up. He smelled magic being used.

One of the cats roared.

Stuart found the strand of magic he wanted. He pulled it towards him. He felt the energy beneath his hands, like used putty. It might not be as powerful as it was originally, but he could reshape it into what he wanted.

He opened his eyes in time to see Tenny grapple with Drew. She turned him so that his back was to Tom and Stuart. Tom moved slightly so that Stuart had a clear line. The bond-mates were telling them what was happening.

Stuart threw a bolt of energy at the back of Drew's neck. It might break it but at that point, he didn't care.

Drew's head snapped forward. Stuart watched as the energy was reabsorbed into Drew's body. Still, it slowed him for a moment.

Kayley moved in and kicked him in the knees.

Drew spun, his weight on one foot, and sent a bolt of ice at Kayley. Someone, probably Amber, threw up a shield around the girl, but Stuart watched as it pierced her flesh, blood flowing freely down her left side.

As Kayley fell, she backed into the Christmas tree, bringing it down nearly on top of her. She rolled out from beneath it just in time to avoid being buried beneath the plastic limbs and ornaments, many of which shattered on the floor around her.

Tom kicked out at Drew's other leg, knocking him to the ground. Tenny kicked him in the side. Stuart added magic to the pummeling.

Drew was down and no longer fighting back. Stuart paused, wondering if they'd gone too far and injured their clowder-mate, perhaps killing him once more.

A scream from one of the cats echoed behind him, by the door.

Amber felt Minnett's mind join with hers as she wove shielding spells around the clowder. Minnett guided her in repurposing the spells she used to stop a body from losing blood into spells that shielded. Once Amber understood the idea, it was easier.

It didn't keep Kayley from getting speared with an ice spear, but at least the thing wasn't sticking out her back. Instead, she rested on the floor, surrounded by shards of broken glass and plastic from the Christmas tree.

Grey and Riley were busy with the two witches at the front door. Those two were hard to focus on. Any time they turned and the figure hit the light, it reflected back into Amber's eyes almost like metal. Grey and Riley didn't appear affected by that.

Mack, now an oversized tiger, had been thrown against the wall. He panted hard, but hadn't lost his size. Whatever wounds he had taken weren't that serious.

"Move to the side, again," Minnett ordered.

Boyd and Chara, now both oversized Siamese, Chara

nearly the same size as the normally larger Boyd, leaped down the stairs. They weren't quite as large as Mack had gotten but were at least lion-sized. Boyd's heavier muscled body was broader than Chara's though their backs were nearly the same height.

While both flew towards the ice figures, Boyd turned his body in mid-leap, avoiding a blast of ice that flew towards him. He landed on the other side of the railing. Chara was hit but she let her momentum carry her towards the ice figure to the right.

Amber expected to hear ice shattering but there was only a hard thump as Chara landed on the ground. She backed up, limping a little. Blood dripped from her shoulder, the dark red smearing her beige fur.

Boyd had moved around the corner to work with Tom and Tenny who were now fighting Chase. With Drew down, Tenny and Stuart disappeared from Amber's view, probably going to join the two men fighting against Chase. Fin, Matt, and Anson rounded the corner to help take on the frost witches.

Above her, Cari and Julia stood. Julia carried a compound bow and metal arrows. Amber smelled garlic. They'd spent the time painting the tips with garlic butter. It worked for Courtney. She wondered if the arrows themselves were silver.

Amber remembered Julia getting a package of something a week or so ago and being spectacularly happy about it. Courtney and she had talked. Maybe the tips were silver or they were just talking about the potential of arrows taking down the frost witches.

"*Duck,*" Minnett said. "*Julia is good with a bow but she is not in practice, not since earlier this summer.*"

Amber wondered why she hadn't known Julia practiced with a bow.

"You don't take an interest in that kind of thing," Minnett said. Amber felt the low purr from the cat. Those that hadn't leaped into the fray were creating a spell for the house. Low and uneven, Amber didn't recognize the tones.

The arrow shot over Amber's head and flew true, hitting the same figure Chara had gone after. Ice slowed the arrow but it flew through the shield and hit the figure, though the ice didn't shatter.

A half-second later, the arrow dropped to the floor, no apparent damage done.

Another arrow flew.

More ice. In fact, this time, Amber felt the cold arctic blast flowing over her. Her teeth began to chatter. Even as her muscles got sore and tired from the chattering, Amber's body began to feel as if it weighed a thousand pounds. She needed to rest.

"Get off the stairs," Minnett ordered.

Amber crawled up one step. The stairs felt higher. Normally it was easy to move a foot up each riser, but now she felt as if she had gone mountain climbing.

The second step was harder than the first. She needed to go to sleep.

Someone pulled at her arm, practically dragging her up.

Loud purring surrounded her. Warmth surged around her, sinking into her chilled flesh. She pushed herself to her hands and knees and got to the top of the stairwell. Cari was with her, shivering, but she had a blanket wrapped around her.

She pulled Amber to her. Julia was shaking beneath a heavy winter coat and a blanket, but she was attempting to stand and shoot another arrow. The smell of garlic was thicker there. Amber noticed the jar of minced garlic on the ground. They'd been coating the arrows.

Amber was barely able to think. Around her the purring paused, leaving her bereft of even that small comfort.

Axel came out with Wheelie right behind him. The two were nearly as big as Mack.

They didn't leap down the stairs so much as stalk down them. The purrs began again and became lower, practically below her hearing. Amber had a hard time focusing on Axel and Wheelie.

Amber doubted the ice figures had any issues seeing the cats. They were more powerful than any of the rest of them.

Still, she watched, hoping Axel and Wheelie would manage to take one out. Axel swiped with his paw, drawing the figure's attention. As the figure sent a blast of cold towards Axel, Wheelie leaped into the fray, knocking it down.

Shards of ice shattered on the floor.

Both cats went after the figure fighting against Grey and Riley, which now moved slower than Amber remembered.

Wheelie went flying towards the living room, out of Amber's line of sight. She wanted to stand up and see, but she was very tired.

Axel was hit next and knocked into Riley and Grey. Amber lost sight of Grey's head but Riley stood up again almost immediately.

Before she knew what happened, Julia had let another arrow fly, which embedded itself in the ice figure's chest.

No shattering, but the ice started to crack.

Mack got up and swiped at it, while the witch was distracted keeping her figure together. The ice shattered on the ground.

Grey sent the shards scattering out the door before turning around. Amber knew he was going to fight Chase.

"How are the fighters?" Amber thought to Minnett.

"*Injured, all of them. I can feel Wheelie but he's not conscious. I suspect he damaged his ribs. He's already losing his size. Of everyone he is hurt the worst.*" Minnett said.

Amber dragged herself up. She had to get to the cat.

COURTNEY

Courtney acted on instinct or perhaps Dawn's knowledge. She pulled energy from anything sent at her and then used as little as possible to take Chase out. Dawn knew the frost witches tended to play with their opponents. Best if they played back.

When the bond-mates and the bond-mate cats managed to destroy the figures of the two frost witches, Courtney saw Riley sweep the shards out the door and let it slam. The house quieted. It was up to her, Anson, and Fin against Chase. Riley and Grey needed to recharge.

Drew was down. Tom was examining him. Tenny had run to the other room.

Courtney didn't smell death, though having never smelled it before, she couldn't be sure why she knew that. Still, Drew's scent hadn't changed, nor had Wheelie's, though both were down. At least Wheelie obviously breathed, even if it did seem too shallow and rapid to her untrained eye.

Anson spun back and hit the door.

"Chase," Courtney said.

The creature inside Chase looked at her and sneered. "You are weak."

Courtney knew that. The insult didn't bother her. She'd fought off two other frost witches. She and Dawn had paired. She used Dawn's knowledge. Dawn used her creativity. Together they were more powerful than apart.

The comfortable beige sofa that she loved napping on had been overturned. The rug in the main room had even been turned up. At some point, she'd registered the crash of the Christmas tree from the front room, the shattering of dozens of ornaments.

Fin leaned on the bo stick, though he was ready to defend. Boyd stalked Chase, bits of ice sticking to his toes and even his whiskers.

Mack padded in behind Courtney. He moved too slowly for a big cat. He, too, panted, but kept his size. He sat near Courtney, protecting her. Grey, shorter than Courtney now, and barely solid, limped into the room.

Courtney felt him pulling energy. She avoided sipping from it, though she ached to do so. Dawn would have if Courtney hadn't held her in check. She would be someone who picked food from another's plate without asking.

Chase took that moment to draw energy. Courtney felt him attempt to siphon it from Mack and Boyd. Courtney cut off that feast.

Glaring at her, Chase half-closed his eyes, clearly searching for another place to draw energy from. Courtney let Dawn follow him, drawing energy from his sources, the first one a middle-aged couple snuggling on the sofa in front of the television. Dawn drew from the electrical energy, while Chase drew from the humans. Dawn sipped from his stream while drinking in as much as she could from the power grid.

The television went out suddenly.

Chase left that house and went to the next one. Only the refrigerator and furnace ran there. Someone was curled up under a blanket, reading a book. Courtney smelled illness. Still, Chase drew from them. Encouraged them subtly to be angry about their illness. Then he and Dawn fed easily from the emotions, taking little life force.

Emotions and electricity never quite did it. The life force held aspects of both combined. That was to be savored.

Courtney felt Chase get hit with something. She focused on the room she was in, on what was around her. Julia had come down and shot him with one of her garlic tipped arrows. They'd talked about what to use a week or so ago. Dawn hadn't had any input but Courtney had felt the reactions. She had no fear of silver, didn't really understand what it was, but she did not like garlic. Garlic wasn't without energy, but there was something about the way it worked as a healing herb that bothered her. It was hard to break down to feed on.

The smell blocked other scents, blinding a hunter, creating shadows for the frost witches against other energies. Not so much a cure as a deterrent.

Still, the arrow hurt Chase's physical body. Julia had gotten him in the left thigh, on the outside. Only a few drops of blood fell.

The smell bothered the frost witch. It sent a blast of cold air towards them. Courtney and Grey stepped in front, taking in the energy of the ice, letting the magic of it replenish their stores while Chase depleted his own.

Julia shot another arrow, which Chase deflected. He raised a hand and spun Courtney, Grey, and Julia around.

Just as she went sprawling, Courtney saw Mack leap at Chase. Then Boyd.

She heard someone fall, didn't think it was her.

Then, her head banged against the floor, sending a shock of pain through her neck and back.

Darkness threatened at the edges of her vision.

Dawn drank in the pain, turning that pain into energy, feeding on it, even as it began to ramp up. The pain started to drill so deeply into Courtney's body that she thought she'd vomit.

It passed then, Dawn easing off on her feeding.

Courtney sat up. Everyone was down.

Chase knelt, head down, eyes closed.

"Chase?" she whispered.

Chase raised his head. His eyes were pained. Mack lay in a heap near him, shrinking quickly. Courtney noted the blood.

"I think I killed him," Chase whispered and then began to cry.

Courtney crawled to the cat and laid her hand on his side. He lived but he was so weak. She fed what energy she could to him, much like she'd fed into Drew's lifeless body, hoping that energy would heal him.

His breathing evened out.

Amber walked slowly in. She was too injured to help much, but Courtney backed off, letting her take care of things.

Stuart went to Chase and pulled the arrow out of his leg. Courtney wanted to protest hoping the garlic on the tip would keep the frost witch from returning.

She didn't feel the witches around the house. They'd gone to lick their wounds.

"We have to go soon," Grey said. "Get them at the portal."

Riley limped in. She leaned against the sofa. Courtney wasn't sure if it was really Riley or someone from Cat Home. When Riley straightened and let her eyes close, Courtney sensed her search for energy. Still not their Riley, but apparently some physical problems resisted even the energies of possession.

"We need to recharge," Riley said softly. "The cats are injured. I'm not sure we can do it without them."

Courtney agreed.

"They'll be equally injured and tired," Grey protested. "Now is the time. If we can get them to the portal…"

"We could be killed there as well as them," Riley said. "I needed rest even before they came."

"We're down at least two cats," Amber said. "There's no way Mack and Wheelie can go back out. That's going to be a distraction for Julia."

"Boyd is waking," Tenny said. "I think he's going to be okay."

Courtney felt some argument among the cats.

Stuart looked up. "An hour. We regroup for an hour. Humans and cats get food and a nap. Grey can do what he does. Riley and Courtney can eat and recoup."

Riley glanced at him as if food were beneath her.

"You're in a human body," Stuart said. "Trust me. You need food as much as you need to draw life force."

Amber worked on Mack. Courtney felt the energy pouring into him. The fact that Dawn hungered to draw from that energy, told her how tired she was. Courtney pushed herself to her feet to get food. Julia was already in the kitchen along with Fin. Even Anson had pushed himself up.

Sodas and fruit juice were passed around. Someone got bread and meats and a sandwich line was made. Courtney hoped this was the last time she had to do this, at least for a very long time. She felt like she'd just run a marathon and was expected to do another one after she got a bite to eat.

She didn't know how much more she could handle.

CHASE

Thrust back into his body, Chase thought someone had stabbed him with a hot poker. He looked down at his leg, at the arrow sticking out. Mack was practically on his lap, the cat's body lying at an awkward angle, Chase's hands buried in the fur near his neck.

He pulled his hands away and bent over, sobbing.

Mack still radiated warmth. His body moved ever so slightly under Chase. Courtney knelt down and fed energy to the cat. Chase watched as the cat's chest began to take in more air as he breathed.

Amber came over, moving more slowly than he would have expected, to help Mack. Her eyes looked sunken with gray shadows circling them. Chase scooted away, setting off the fire in his thigh.

He looked at the arrow. Stuart came over, looking at Chase's leg. Stuart knelt down and stared at it in the way he did, with eyes appearing to look at something well behind Chase, except, of course, there was nothing behind the leg except the floor.

Stuart pulled the arrow out. Chase would have sworn he

heard a rip. Blood splattered around them like fine scarlet raindrops. Fire burned up his thigh to his chest. Chase gasped.

No wonder the damned frost witch had left him. No one would want to feel that pain if they didn't have to. Deep down, Chase knew the witch could have healed him if it had wanted to. Instead, it had fled.

Looking around at the dragging bodies, the haunted eyes, the cats still standing—all of them looked wiped out. This was worse than the fights they'd had before.

For himself, Chase might have allowed Drew to die, but he couldn't bear the thought of killing one of the cats. He felt particularly bad that it was Mack he nearly killed. First Drew. Then his bond-mate.

The others discussed resting versus going back out after the frost witches. Grey was all for going out right then. No matter that his form shimmered in Chase's eyes, as if he couldn't even remain human-looking. Chase didn't let himself wonder what Grey really looked like. He knew he wouldn't like it. If it was pleasing, Grey wouldn't have wasted the energy to look human.

It didn't stop Grey from grabbing food from the island where Julia, Cari, Tenny, and Tom were making up sandwiches for the group. Anson sat on the floor across the room from Chase. He leaned against the wall next to the fireplace. Chase didn't understand why he could see through the sofa and only then realized it had been tipped over and was angled oddly.

No one had started putting the furniture back together. They were just trying to eat, planning a raid on the frost witches.

"Take me when you go," Chase said. "When I feel her leap into me, I'll jump through the portal."

Stuart said nothing. He kept wiping at the wound.

Chase wondered if he'd even spoken aloud.

Stuart looked up at him. "We're discussing it. Trag has some say in this, too."

As if the cat was more important than he was. Chase wanted to get mad. Couldn't quite achieve it. He knew why they were talking to Trag. He might still be under the influence of the witch, even if it had temporarily fled his body.

Chase's mind felt empty to him without the frost witch lurking in the corners, ready to take over and destroy something or someone he loved. It ate up the pain he often felt when it did that. The creature had loved his guilt over Drew, the guilt that drug out for far longer than even the frost witch expected. An unexpected feast, though emotions were like cream to the creature, they weren't that filling, not like life force.

Amber sat back from Mack. The cat looked better. His fur seemed smoother and he breathed more easily. She limped over to Boyd, who waited not far away. All the cats Chase could see were normal-sized. Most were in the kitchen, being fed. Even the ones who hadn't charged into the fray, like Trag, had been using magic.

Chase closed his eyes against the pressure Stuart placed on the wound as he wrapped it. His stomach growled, or maybe it was Stuart's.

The purr magic had sung to him while he'd been at his lake. He'd felt it there, warming the air. He'd felt stronger than normal, almost as if he could have taken over his own body. He hadn't tried, though. He should have tried but he knew the pain the witch could inflict.

Chase wondered about what would have happened if he'd tried to fight the witch. Maybe Amber could be resting instead of healing Mack. Chara was wounded, too, as was Wheelie. She could be healing them first instead of having to come over and work on Mack. Chase closed his eyes.

His stomach growled, again. Stuart left him, the bandage wrapped around his upper thigh. Amber would need to clean it further, but that could wait. Others needed energetic healing far more than he needed a clean wound. Chase didn't know if anyone would care if he died.

He sat there in a half stupor, berating himself for all the things he'd left undone until someone gave him a soda and a sandwich, which he ate. It tasted like sawdust in his mouth but he ate anyway. The soda perked him up as well.

Everyone was lying back and napping on the floor, looking like so many broken marionettes. Even Grey lay on the floor.

Chase tried to keep his eyes open, afraid that the witch would make an appearance if he let himself go. His body felt cold and hot at the same time. He thought that was a sign of shock. He really ought to ask Amber.

Before long, Chase was lying on his back, eyes closing as sleep enveloped him.

S tuart rested as much as he could. He'd used a lot of magic to shore up shields and lend support for energy and ice blasts. He'd helped the cats maintain their large shapes. He fell asleep on the floor of Fin's room where there was a spot of carpet which was too thin to do much against the hardness of the wood.

Pushing himself up, feeling every second of his age as if he were purely human, Stuart looked around. The light was dim. Fin stirred in the bed, a light blanket wrapped over him. They'd all been exhausted.

Grey had agreed to Stuart's suggestion of an hour of rest. Stuart knew why he was awake right then. Grey wanted it. Fin would get up when he needed to. Stuart didn't push the younger man. Everyone needed as much rest as possible.

"*How are the cats?*" Stuart thought to Trag, including Trag in the question.

"*Mack is resting on Drew's bed, along with Wheelie,*" Trag said. "*Vitals are good, though their energy is lower than we'd like. Wheelie has a damaged hind leg and several vertebrae out of align-ment. Amber moved as much as she could, but she was worn out trying to add shields to help stand against the witches. Chara can fight, though she's wounded."*

"And the people?"

"Exhausted, generally. Kayley won't be able to fight. She's on the sofa in the front room. Amber wanted to get her to the medic room but neither of them had the energy to go down the stairs."

Trag's voice echoed all the fatigue that Stuart felt.

Stuart made his made to the great room. Though silver hurricane shutters covered the windows, the lights in the room felt bright. Julia, Cari, and Courtney were curled on the rug in front of the gas fireplace, which was lit. Someone had pulled down a blanket. Axel curled on it with them, Wheelie lay just above Julia's head, probably placed there by someone else. Navy, Wilbur, and Trag all encircled him. Stuart could almost hear their purrs. Normal cat purrs but even those sounds were the frequency at which bone healed.

Courtney sat up when he walked out. Riley was at the kitchen counter snacking. She met his eyes but said nothing. She didn't even nod. The cat home representative was still in residence.

"The others from Cat Home?" Stuart asked quietly.

He heard a groan. Chase was on the floor between the kitchen and the breakfast area.

"Another hour, maybe," Riley said. "They're working hard so won't be at full power. We need to be ready to go now. I can feel the frost witches growing in power."

Grey joined them in the kitchen. He'd made no noise coming down the stairs, but from the tidiness of his clothing and hair, he'd gone up to sleep on a real bed. It even appeared as if he'd taken the time to splash water on his face.

Stuart yawned and grabbed a soda. He didn't normally enjoy them very often but the sugars in it, plus the caffeine would boost his ability to think.

"They are getting restless again," Grey said. "I expect

they'll take over Chase first. Drew is far more injured. Two broken ribs, a slight concussion…"

Stuart didn't want to think about what they'd done to Drew.

"He's already been brought back from the dead once," Riley said calmly. "We never tried that on a human before."

They sounded like they were talking about science experiments. Comments like that were what bothered Stuart about Base Command. At Cat Home, at least, there had been less of that. Probably because they were on good behavior for him, feeding him the information he would need and letting his cells absorb it, even as they absorbed the ability to change, though Stuart had yet to find out how he was changing.

Tom and Tenny came in from the front room. Anson and Matt followed, though Anson was limping.

"Anson should stay here," Grey said. "Someone needs to stay with Amber and Kayley."

The others, worn out as they were, would go along.

"What about the snow?" Cari asked. She yawned as she stretched. She stood near where she'd been lying down.

"We'll create a shield," Riley said. "I have fed well and am more myself."

"I have also re-upped the energy I need," Grey said.

Courtney hung her head but she nodded. Stuart searched for energy from the land. He felt nothing at all. He'd never felt such a dead area. Everything had some sort of energy but not this land, not anymore. Even the house felt vulnerable, a shack of sticks and twigs and not a home of lumber and brick.

Stuart wandered to the kitchen, grabbing some fruit and nuts to munch on. Fin entered the great room. He looked exhausted, but he stood upright.

When everyone was in the room, even Amber, who must

have been sleeping in the living room, Grey clapped his hands once to get attention.

Stuart noted the cats were all alert and watching. He felt the presence of Mack and Wheelie from the other room.

"I'll create a shield. We'll all go in a group up to the portal," Grey said. "Amber, Anson, and Kayley will stay here with the following bond-mates: Mack, Wheelie, Minnett, Anastasia."

"We'll need coats," Courtney added. She yawned. No matter that she'd had energy, her human body needed rest. A different type of energy than could be siphoned or else she and Dawn hadn't been able to reach far enough to gather more energy.

Stuart waited while the others, slower than he was, shuffled out to the closet to grab a coat. Chase pushed himself up. Stuart frowned.

"You aren't going," Amber snapped at Chase.

"Yes," Courtney said, "He is. You can't protect yourself against him if the witch leaps back into him. We need to take him along."

Tom went out to the garage. He came back a few minutes later with a pair of ski poles that Chase could use as walking sticks.

Courtney got Chase's jacket.

"What about Drew?" Anson asked.

"We'll make sure he gets there," Riley said.

Stuart was the last one to the closet. He grabbed his heavy coat, the one that fell midway to his knees, and buttoned it. He had a pair of light gloves and heavier ski gloves in the pockets. He pulled on his hat. The shielding might help them against the snow, keeping them from being influenced such that they didn't know where to go, but he doubted that anything would help the cold.

With the broken glass in the door, even the house was

cold. He was surprised anyone had been able to sleep in the living room.

Each person picked up one of the bond-mate cats, their own when possible. Riley and Grey held Drew between them. Stuart smelled the faint traces of magic that let them hold him up in such a way that it almost appeared he was walking on his own.

They were ready to go. When the door opened, Stuart shivered at the chill out there. He understood that going to the portal would make it possible to push the witches through it, to keep them from finding this world with any ease, but he wasn't looking forward to making that stand. The only good news was that if they failed, the rest of the group from Cat Home who was on their way would get there too soon for the witches to have completely re-grouped.

As he walked out onto the porch, waiting for Riley or Grey to create a shield, Stuart wondered if the others felt like they were about to walk down their own death row.

CHASE

Chase dressed warmly. His leg was bandaged and he wasn't sure how he'd walk all the way to the park where the portal was. Once upon a time, he and Trag would go out and walk up the street, the cat following him. Anyone in the neighborhood watching would have seen a man walking with his black cat following him.

A little girl named Natalie lived a few doors up and was often out on her driveway drawing hopscotch patterns or riding her bike under her mom's eye. She'd always ask if she could pet Trag. Trag would pause to let her give him chin scratches and rub his back carefully. Chase always wondered what her mom thought about him going for a walk with his cat.

Other days, he'd jog and Trag would join him in the run. He'd never cared what others thought of him because he had Trag and if they wanted to run, they ran. The telepathic link meant Chase never had to worry about Trag being lost. Even if something did try to hurt him, an unleashed dog who wanted to run after a cat, well, Trag had his magic, as did Chase.

It had been months since he'd been able to go to the park. He was out of shape from having only the basement room in which to exercise. It wasn't like he couldn't have worked out doing Pilates or some such thing but Chase liked hiking and being outdoors. Exercising to stay in shape didn't interest him.

As a result, he worried about the walk, worried he'd hold them back, particularly with the wound in his leg. They'd shot him with an arrow.

Other than the bandage and making sure he got some antibiotics, they hadn't done any healing on him. Chase didn't blame them. Amber was worn out with all she had to do. Kayley needed more healing. The cats, particularly Mack, needed far more healing than he had gotten but at least he was stable. Chase was thankful for that.

Riley and Grey were basically zombie-walking Drew to the park. He was far worse off than Chase. Chase hoped that with the injuries Drew sustained that he was at least remaining unconscious. The pain of being held upright would be excruciating with the broken ribs and the concussion he had to have considering the blood that dripped from his scalp.

The frost witches wouldn't care. Chase knew that it would be nearly as easy to reanimate a dead body as to take over a living one. It just wouldn't be satisfying as a dead person had no emotion. The only energy would come from the decomposition and not the turning of food and air into cellular energy. But, for a short time, dead bodies would work. Long term, not nearly as well.

Chase watched Stuart carrying Trag down the road. Trag rested on Stuart's forearm, his butt tucked in near Stuart's elbow and pressed against his side. Being held cuddled like that no doubt kept him warmer than Chase.

While there was no wind, the cold pressed in against him

making his nose feel dry and his lungs hurt with each breath. Muscles in his thigh ached with each step and the only reason he hadn't fallen was thanks to the ski poles.

The houses around them sat silent, barely in view. Night had fallen while they rested and if the night wasn't dark enough, fog pressed against them. Falling snow slid off the shield around them which acted as a giant invisible umbrella. Even so, the damp seeped into Chase's body, chilling him further.

No one was talking. The snow absorbed the sounds of their feet so only the soft sounds of cloth rubbing against cloth sounded. Even those sounds were eaten by the snow and clouds.

Chase imagined the clouds eating the sounds. He wondered if sounds held any energy for the clouds, energy that the frost witches might then take from the clouds. One big circle of life. Except that the witches stopped the circle. Instead of feeding anything, they held the energy, using it only to destroy more things and feeding on the destruction, like an animal re-eating food it had vomited up.

Chase had had a cat that did that once. Trag, fortunately, did not. He'd not seen any of the bond-mate cats do such a thing. Of course, if they had an issue with a food, they could just say something. Ordinary cats had no such ability, limited as they were to a vocabulary that consisted of variations of meow.

The pain in his thigh was off the scales before they got to the stop sign. Chase bemoaned the times he'd walked the long block so easily. Yet he'd have fallen down and stopped if not for the poles helping him stay up. Even those barely held him.

They were over halfway there. No tracks marred the surface of the snow. A light was on in the back of the house on the corner. It was the first sign of life Chase had noticed.

The group crossed the street and walked down the sidewalk. Riley prodded him nearly every step to keep up. Though Chase was freezing, sweat beaded along his forehead. The world appeared before him beneath shades of blistering red pain.

This side of the street held trees that looked unfamiliar in their white garb. Branches hung so low that they scraped the top of the shield and dropped snow around the group as they walked. Chase breathed harder, the cold air chilling his lungs further. He wanted nothing so much as to get inside and warm his lungs.

Drew's head came up slightly. Chase watched, wondering if Drew had woken up or if it was some sort of bounce reaction to the walk. He didn't feel one of the witches. He thought he would.

"Why here?" Chase panted.

"If we engage them here and we can shatter them, we can send the shards in between worlds before the witches have fled. Even if we get only parts of them, they'll be helpless. Yes, they can re-feed to get energy back but in a world like this it will take decades if not centuries." Riley spoke quietly though her voice sounded flat in the night air.

Chase wanted to ask what they planned to do with him and Drew. He didn't think he'd like the answer, so he stayed silent.

The group, with Grey in the lead, turned into the park. The snow was heavier there, perhaps the parking lot hadn't completely melted off after the last little snow. The only good thing was that Chase's lower legs were so cold that they offset the burning in his injured leg. Besides, if he fell, the snow would be a good cushion.

Grey didn't take the path but walked directly across the grass to the little treed area at the far edge of the park. Snow hung heavy over the place. As he walked, Chase noticed that the portal area held less snow. He thought he saw vague shimmers around it, but they'd change and go away as he looked straight on.

It felt wrong to be there without having Trag connected to him. He'd always seen the portal as much through the cat's eyes as his own. He used to feel the changes in his blood. Now, he felt nothing. Had it bothered Stuart after the loss of his cat?

Chase hadn't thought about the man from Base Command in those terms before. Stuart had always been the enemy, even before he'd tried to get rid of Chase's frost witch. To an extent, Chase understood the clowder still saw him as other. Only the beings from Cat Home were more other than even Stuart, which now made him feel almost like part of the clowder.

Waves of energy hit him as he got closer. Chase realized then that the portal used energy, was made up of energy. It was the perfect feeding spot. They'd come to the waterhole to wait for the predator. Chase knew they wouldn't have long to wait.

Drew turned to look at him, his face strained with pain.

Chase met his gaze. They both knew what they had to do. He hoped at least one of them was brave enough to go through with the plan that each of them had clearly thought of. Both of them had to go through the portal to a place between worlds and die with their frost witch.

COURTNEY

Courtney hadn't noticed the power from the portal, exactly, not until it had been pointed out. Then it was like noticing air. While Dawn had siphoned energy from the land around the portal she hadn't actually taken energy from it.

Dawn had explained earlier that it was dangerous to drink energy from the portal. Now Courtney understood the danger. It would be like drinking heady wine, too easy to take more than you should. Plus, now, they needed to fight, to be in control. To drink from such concentrated energy would allow one to be completely out of control, drunk on the power.

Courtney felt the sense of it in her body, though she wasn't sure she completely understood. The portal drew her with its tasty smorgasbord of energies, the easiness of the drawing.

"It's not easy to use this power," Courtney said out loud, looking from Grey to Riley.

Riley smiled. "But you feel the temptation, don't you? Does your witch strain to drink it in?" Courtney noted there was a level of lust there, waiting for her to sip from it. She didn't quite know what that would prove to the creatures from Cat Home.

"I do," Courtney admitted. No reason not to. Riley and Grey would be feeling it as well.

Stuart squatted as he placed Trag carefully on the ground. There was little snow there, at least compared to other areas. Still, Grey had kept up the shield. The energy of that was probably as tempting as the portal and far less dangerous.

Courtney admired the gentle way Stuart handled the cat. While she'd learned to not just tolerate cats but to rather like them—at least these—she wasn't sure she'd ever have a cat even if she got out of this alive. Dogs still held a special place in her heart. Dogs wouldn't remind her of the pain of this time.

If she'd have been fully human, she'd never have noticed the slight drop in temperature as the frost witches appeared. Already her breath fogged the air, though her lungs didn't burn the way she thought they should have. Courtney knew she was lucky to have Dawn taking care of her, mingled with her own body and soul so that they were more than one or the other.

The frost witches barely appeared, icy shimmers in the darkness, when Courtney felt Dawn reach out to break off one of the heavy branches and let it fall towards the witches.

One shattered easily.

Instead of having time to toss the shards through the portal, Courtney noted the energy flowing to Chase.

He changed subtly, standing taller.

His eyes took in the clowder around him. While the area closest to the portal had little snow, the rest of the park more. Snow rose up around them and began to whirl. Courtney noted the soft flakes hardening into ice. How fine-tuned her senses had become.

Dawn took such knowledge for granted. She was frustrated by the limits of the poor eyesight, smell, and hearing of a human. She had far more admiration for the bond-mate cats than humans. In her world, the world she remembered, humans wouldn't have been chosen to bond.

Courtney and Dawn used more wind, blowing outward, to disturb the pattern of the swirling snow.

As it dissipated, Courtney noted the frost witches had solidified into blobs that shone faintly blue. Vaguely oval in shape, not quite opaque, they hung in the air. Courtney tingled from the magic pulsing within them.

This wasn't the true form of the creatures, but it allowed them to work with the world more easily than they could when they took human forms.

Courtney had an urge to let her eyes close and lay down near a tree and nap. She noted that Cari was blinking hard against the same thing.

The cats began to purr and Courtney no longer had to concentrate on not falling asleep.

She searched around for creative ways to fight the witches.

While she did that, momentarily paused in doing something, Chase knocked into Grey taking him out. Courtney felt the energy drawn out from the hit as well as the fall.

She ached to help but had no idea how.

The cats grew to larger sizes, the purring changing, becoming deeper.

Riley created a whirlwind of energy around Chase, holding him in place.

As she did so, a shard of ice hit her in the back and she went down. Courtney watched as blood flowed from a wound in her back.

She heard Anastasia's cry deep in her body, an echo of

pain and sorrow. It had to be the telepathic link. Anastasia wasn't even in the park.

Not able to think of anything else, Courtney used the wind on the blobs of frost witches.

They pushed through, though she could have sworn they looked a bit smaller.

Grey pulled himself up. He warmed the ground, melting the snow around them. The landscaped changed to a slight bowl shape and soon enough Courtney was standing ankle-deep in cold water.

Grey let go of the water, leaving behind the slight burnt candle scent of his magic..

Wind had energy and power that could be drawn from. Water was harder, especially water that was near freezing. The frost witches ate the energy of cold as well as heat but temperatures that were neither were more difficult to feed on.

Water held energy, hated to let it go. Dawn had been on a world that was mostly water and had fled. The others hadn't even joined her there for the short time she'd inhabited it.

Courtney spun just as an ice bolt sailed towards her. She watched it shatter. Felt the speed with which it had passed her. The witches were already slightly weaker. They'd started weaker to begin with and now the water was making them work for their energy.

It gave her hope, though she didn't see how they could win. Even with decreased energy, they were stronger than she was. Stronger than Grey.

Chara chewed on Chase's leg, keeping him down. She danced out of the way of the ice bolts he sent towards her, though her fur was covered in ice crystals.

Trag danced around, just out of reach, making Chase attempt to throw ice at him. Heat radiated from Chase's hand at one point, singeing a tail.

Courtney smelled burnt fur. All of the clowder appeared uncertain. Drew sat on the ground. He continued to try and push himself up but fell twice.

Courtney pictured a bowling ball of water and sent hurtling towards the frost witch closest to her.

Watched as it got closer.

Stuart was ready with an energetic broom-like form to sweep shards through the portal.

The ball hit.

The broom swept shards before they'd barely detached and sent them through the portal.

Courtney saw black light flashes out of the corner of her eye.

She tossed another bowling bowl at the next witch, but her watery bowling ball veered around it, easily, smacking into one of the trees.

The frost witches always learned.

STUART

Stuart watched the bowling ball Courtney and Dawn had created of energy and water. The first one had worked. He hadn't been certain it would. The witch could as easily have absorbed the energy of it into their blob shape as be shattered by it.

The blob shape wasn't made from ice, but it could be injured.

Julia shot her arrows, the tips still covered in garlic. Stuart continued to hate the smell.

Except for the cats purring and the occasional grunt or groan, they fought in silence.

Axel and Shahanna enlarged and crouched, waiting for a moment to leap and attack. The witches weren't the only ones who learned.

Stuart held on to his energetic broom, waiting. Even that was a potential weapon.

He feinted at the witches a few times, hoping it would distract them. They learned so quickly though. Each trick and feint had to be new.

Stuart's eyes began to feel heavy. He examined his energetic body, unsurprised to find a shadow snake leaching it from him.

He pulled it off, feeling better almost immediately.

Just as quickly shadows flew at him on the energetic plane. They danced around him, weaving into a dark web, holding him there.

Stuart tested the web with an energetic finger, felt it try to grab him and hold him.

He held still, changing his broom into an energetic chainsaw which he used to saw through the web.

Unfortunately, he underestimated the stickiness of the web, which held onto the saw and grew around it, the sticky strands edging closer to his hands.

Stuart dropped the energetic chainsaw. He watched as the energy he'd used to create the tool was gobbled up by a hungry frost witch.

He swore. Maybe aloud. Maybe not.

Fire was the next option. Stuart created an energetic image of what he thought a flame thrower might look like. It was a larger form of a rifle, broad and round. On the energetic plane, though it was large and awkward, it had no weight.

Stuart fired it at the web, burning through the magic.

The witch ate up the energy, but not as fast as Stuart could burn through it.

He made an opening for himself and slipped out of the plane before the frost witch could trap him.

Axel was down, bleeding from his back. Julia was screaming as she shot her arrows, which were nearly gone.

Courtney had fallen to the ground.

Tenny was fighting with a baseball bat, hitting at the blobs, and dancing back. Her face was covered in white frost and she breathed hard.

Matt was lying near the portal an arm outstretched.

Riley curled in a ball, bleeding from her back where an ice shard continued to melt.

Stuart watched as something large and icy stepped through the portal. It was a figure like a golem, but made of ice. It pushed against the portal edges as it stepped through. Energy slipped out of the portal and was drawn into the figure.

Either another frost witch had shown up or this was the one he had sent to the between, back to help the others.

Courtney groaned as she sat up. She was pale, but Grey shimmered in the portal's faint light, as if he were only half-there.

Just then, Drew stood up, limped towards the thing, as if he could actually save them.

Drew's body ached all over. He knew he wasn't thinking clearly. In fact, thinking at all challenged him. He probably had a broken rib or two given how much it hurt to breathe. His low back ached. His feet hurt. The headache threatened to make his head explode.

Thankfully, he hadn't been awake for the move to the park. Small favors. They'd let him drop to the ground, not hard, of course. If he'd been an airplane, the pilot would have made a perfect landing. But Drew was bruised flesh and even the gentle landing had jarred him awake.

He'd been surprised to see that he was in front of the portal. For a moment he'd feared they were going to send him through, along with Chase. But seeing Chase, seeing the slight nod, Drew understood they were here in case the frost witches inhabited them again. For some reason, the clowder had come to the portal.

Without having Mack bonded to him, Drew didn't see much in front of him. The area was oddly free of snow.

When everyone started fighting, he hadn't even seen the

witches. Now and then a shadow fell over the group but he'd just laid there, trying to figure out what was going on.

The cats had purred and then grown, still purring, the feeling of their purrs changing with their size. Drew had no doubt the cats all remained on the side of the clowder, uninfected. While the witches generally preferred still air, whirlwinds came up, tiny tornados that whipped around them.

Courtney was down. Stuart frozen, staring into space before coming to and looking around.

The portal shimmered a bit in front of Drew's eyes. A giant ice sculpture of a man walked through. Smoothly formed, it glistened even in the near darkness, only the faint light from the recently used portal to show where it stood. Its feet were the length of Drew's thigh, and Drew wasn't a small man.

He'd been attempting to push himself up, but his arms didn't work quite right. Finally, he stood, legs unsteady. Blood pumped too quickly from his heart which beat too fast. Breathing hurt his lungs and the strain of standing made him breathe even faster.

Pain from his ribs merged with the pain from the cold air and his chest was one big orchestra of aches.

Drew stumbled forward, not certain what he was going to do. Maybe he hoped that the frost witch would take him over and he could stumble through the portal before the witch left his body. Perhaps he could push the ice creature through the portal with him, though given his much smaller size, Drew didn't hold out a lot of hope. Still, it was what he could do. A tiny bit of effort on his part, a small hope that he could be useful in his last moments.

The cold ate away at him as he reached the creature, arms flung out, trying to push it back. Maybe he'd surprise it.

Instead, Drew felt himself falling into a lake of ice.

Shadows swam around him as he sank into the dark

depths. They changed from shadowy ribbons to sharks. Fear crept through his body.

He'd been dead once before. Drew didn't think it would matter too much if he died again. There wasn't a whole lot left of him, to be honest.

The shadow sharks started eating away at his flesh.

The icy depths kept him from feeling the pain of their teeth ripping him apart.

Drew closed his eyes, trying not to think about the sharks destroying him.

He felt nothing but the coldness around him.

Longing for heat, Drew pictured a fire burning in front of him, curling up and warming himself.

The chill started to fade just a bit.

Drew opened his eyes.

He wasn't in the cold depths of the lake. He was in a cabin with a fire going. He sat on a low ottoman in front of the fire. A patterned quilt lay over his legs.

A broken old man sat in a chair next to him.

Next to Drew, near the fire, lay a creature that looked half-dog, half-shark. It had ears and no gills, though the nose was all shark.

"What is this place?" Drew asked.

"I was once what you call a frost witch," the old man said. "But in digesting creatures such as yourself I am something other. Like your Courtney is becoming."

"Have you eaten me?" Drew asked.

"Not intentionally," the old man said. "I absorbed you when you tried to push me through into the between. I'd already absorbed the shards of the frost witch sent through moments before."

The old man smiled. In the firelight, his teeth seemed to glow slightly red, as if he'd rended the frost witch the way the sharks had gotten Drew.

Drew tried not to show the fear that ate at him. He didn't want to give this man and his shark-dog the satisfaction.

"I try not to be as greedy as they. The specimen I merged with was, I guess you'd say, emotional, an empath. Emotions are essentially energy, so they, or we, were taken quickly, dying fast. I struggled against destruction, a tiny pebble that wouldn't go away with the witch inside me, merging and changing. I grabbed onto others as they were destroyed, pulling them into me. Now I am more than a pebble. I am a force to be reckoned with. Energy comes to me and I say how to use it."

The man slammed down a cane that appeared in his hand.

"How will you use it here?" Drew asked.

"The frost witches are gobbling energy from your friends, but I am gobbling the witches. Your world isn't as energy-rich as many. There is little magic except what has been placed here. However, you people attach to their emotions. They think of themselves as their emotions feeding that energy over and over again." The old man rocked. "They will provide a satisfying few centuries for the witches."

"You have to stop them!" Drew said.

"I have to eat them," the old man said. "I can only eat so much at once."

Drew thought about how much energy he could take. He imagined himself eating a huge amount of food.

The old man smiled. The shark-dog gave a sort of bark that came out like a snarl, its head up, tail thumping against the hearth.

Drew wanted to wipe that smile off the old man's face. He stood up, surprised he didn't hurt any longer.

He took a few steps towards the old man and slammed his fist into the man's face as hard as he could.

The bones crunched beneath his fist. Warm blood splattered against his face and chest. The shark-dog whined behind him.

Drew looked at his fist in shock. He stepped back, expecting the old man to grow a new head. Instead, the body slumped down in the chair, the blanket falling to the ground.

Turning, Drew looked at the fire. Still burning. The shark-dog whined again, looking up at him.

Drew wanted, no *needed*, to know what was happening.

As soon as the thought occurred to him, he found himself standing near the portal. His view was higher than it should have been, by a couple of feet. Energy from the frost witches assailed him, tasting of blood, and hope, terror, and pain. Anger tasted sweet against his tongue.

The cats fought on. Drew looked for Mack. Didn't see him. Was thankful he wasn't there.

He reached out and grabbed one of the frost witches. The blob slipped from his grasp. Worse than trying to grab a fish from a river, the blob was like a slippery glop of slime swimming in water. Squeeze too hard and it would ooze out. Don't squeeze hard enough and it would float right off his fist.

Drew stepped closer, nearly landing on Tenny, who leaped back at the last minute. She stared up, not recognizing him.

Not being recognized, being looked at like he was evil saddened him.. The frost witch, of course, devoured his sorrow. Drew added his face, the way he remembered it from mirrors on the ice golem he inhabited, hoping his friends would recognize him..

Tenny nodded, turned, and swung the bat at the nearest blob.

Drew grabbed before it slithered just out of reach. This time he didn't let it go. He brought it to his mouth and swallowed.

He nearly gagged. He hated oysters and this creature was like eating an oyster that tasted of rancid oil and rotten eggs. Still, once it was down his throat, Drew felt stronger. He also returned to his cabin, probably because that was a safe place in this new construct that he inhabited.

A witch appeared before him, in a shape that reminded him of Courtney.

The witch attacked him, trying to use magic, but nothing happened. Drew looked over at what was left of the old man in the chair and threw another punch. The witch went down.

Shark-dog howled took large bites from the frost witch's Courtney-like body. Drew shuddered, remembering being eaten in the dark lake. He wondered whether the witch had the same sensation or if it was just gone.

Drew changed his viewpoint again, back to the world outside. Only one frost witch blob remained. And the witch inside Chase.

Drew really didn't want to have to destroy Chase. He really didn't. But he'd do what he had to do to save the clowder.

Courtney's jaw dropped as Drew fell into the giant ice creature. A golem according to Dawn. Maybe not a golem exactly, but Dawn had stolen the term from someone else and it seemed to fit.

When the golem thing scooped up and swallowed one of the frost witches, Courtney gasped.

Dawn was terrified of the creature. Legends about how frost witches were destroyed included a giant creature whose shape changed as easily as their own. Dawn was certain this was that creature. After seeing Drew disappear, Courtney didn't know if she was any safer from it than the frost witches.

Drew's face appeared on the golem, though it wasn't his face exactly. Nicer looking in parts and worse in others. Dawn thought it was how Drew saw himself.

The lone frost witch blob threw bolts of energy at the giant golem. Chase leaped up, though how he managed it, Courtney didn't know. Blood flowed from beneath the bandage on his thigh. The movement had to hurt.

She knew the frost witch inside him wouldn't care. It

could keep functioning, siphoning energy from any pain Chase felt.

Chase used fire to try and drive the golem thing back.

Julia continued firing arrows at the blob. They often hit but didn't stay inside it as the blob changed form, letting them drop to the ground. Courtney thought the blob was moving more slowly.

Navy and Wilbur stalked the blob and tried to spin it towards the golem. They evidently thought that anything that ignored them and went after the frost witches was an ally, at least for the moment.

Grey stood up again, looking more solid and a bit taller. The time he'd been down had let him feed on energy and rebuild himself. He threw an energetic net at the witch. The witch absorbed much of it. Courtney felt the magical energy in the net being taken and used.

The golem's body looked shiny and wet when Chase ran out of fire.

It glanced at Chase, sadness on the face that was almost Drew's.

Courtney knew what had to be done.

She imagined a sword, and an energetic sword appeared in her hand. Deciding it was too large, she created a long knife instead.

As the golem creature bent for the blob, Chase tried to move between the golem's hand and the witch. The blob took that moment to skitter away from the golem with Drew's face.

Courtney threw the long knife, aiming for Chase's other leg, hoping to take him down. The pain might shock the frost witch into letting Chase return.

The knife flew end over end. Courtney imagined it hitting exactly where she wanted.

Her magic made sure her aim was true and the knife

struck the back of Chase's unwounded leg, cutting deeply. His back arched and he screamed in pain.

A fog of energy escaped his body.

The golem opened its mouth and inhaled the fog.

Chase fell to the ground, splashing into a pool of water and landing hard on his back. He writhed in the cold mud, his teeth chattering and his lips going blue.

The golem froze, much as it had after eating the first blob, giving the last of the frost witches a chance to send a bolt of fire at his icy form.

An arm started to melt, the ice turning to water and dripping down into the pool that Grey had made earlier.

Grey and the cats continued to harry the witch, not giving it time to pay too much attention to the golem. The blob changed from oval to round and back again. It appeared to dance, like one of those bouncing dots on a musical score on some cartoon Courtney had watched as a child.

Ice didn't hurt the witch. Fire didn't bother it. Even water only slowed it a little.

Fatigue ate at Courtney.. Stuart had gone over to Riley who continued to bleed and was working on her. It probably was Riley and not the creature from Cat Home. How much longer until the rest of the group from Cat Home got there?

If the golem with Drew's face wasn't actually on their side, they'd need all the help they could get. The clowder was exhausted.

The needles on the evergreens had turned brown and scattered around them. The deciduous trees, leaves long since having fallen, had no more life than the evergreens. Nothing stirred but Courtney and the clowder and the single frost witch.

Giving up seemed like the only option.

Giving in and living in her field of dying flowers would be better than watching all her friends die.

Courtney practically growled. She turned on Dawn who cowered in a corner, equally defeated, though her images were different from Courtney's.

Snow fell around them, touching them.

Their powers were so weak, Courtney could easily be influenced again. So could the others.

Julia ran out of arrows, but instead of running into the fray, she stood there, watching.

Matt kept poking at the creature with a stick, but he was leaning against a tree.

Tenny kicked at it, the blob sinking against her foot. It grabbed at her, and she fell to the side. The blog yanked, dragging her across the field.

The golem woke slowly.

Drew's eyes widened seeing Tenny being dragged. He grabbed the witch blob with one hand and used the other to pull Tenny free. He placed Tenny gently on the ground, even as he squeezed the witch thing before swallowing it whole.

The last frost witch disappeared down the golem's throat.

Once again the golem stopped what it was doing. The clowder waited, muscles tensed. Courtney readied whatever spells she had to try and destroy the creature with Drew's face.

Cari wiped tears from her eyes. Courtney remembered how shattered Kayley had been when Drew had died last time. It was a good thing she'd had to stay behind.

The cats shrank back to their smaller sizes, purring healing spells. Courtney felt her body taking in the healing. Her body became stronger, her mind clearer. She had places where her skin was bruised and frosty. She'd been hit and hadn't noticed.

A creak of ice sounded, loud in the silence. Looking up. Courtney noted the golem studying her. Dawn flinched with fear, and Courtney's heart raced. The golem creature embodied the witch's worst nightmare.

Around her, the snow stopped falling. The sky remained dark as the clouds refused to dissipate.

The golem leaned towards her. Courtney tried to take a step back but her body was frozen in place. She didn't know how long she stood there staring into huge eyes that reminded her of Drew. Her body shook. Dawn cowered.

Courtney tried not to scream as the creature bent closer to her than ever. They had driven the frost witch out of Chase and the golem had eaten it. But Courtney was too entwined with Dawn. The frost witch couldn't leave her.

AMBER

When the door closed and Amber was left with Kayley and Anson, the house felt too quiet. Kayley's shoulder was barely bandaged. Anson had a hard time standing, though Amber hadn't found any obvious wounds.

Amber checked on Mack and Wheelie where they rested in Drew's room. Someone had brought Wheelie down there before the rest of the clowder had left, for which Amber was grateful. The last thing she wanted was more running around.

Then she went downstairs to bring up what she might need for Kayley and Anson. It took several trips to bring it all upstairs from the medic room, but that was easier than trying to help them downstairs. Even so Amber was tired at the end. She needed more rest.

Kayley reclined on the sofa in the front room. Someone had cleared away a spot from the broken ornaments so that Anson could rest on a big blanket with another pulled over him. The chill air breezed through the broken glass of the front door, despite the plastic someone had duct-taped over the window.

Amber dragged out more blankets from Fin's room to cover her patients.

Then she joined the cats in Drew's room and closed her eyes. She needed a minute to breathe. Absently, Amber rubbed Minnett's fur. Both she and Anastasia were curled up with the two most injured cats, purring at them.

"The others are nearing the corner by the park," Minnett told her, with a low purr in the back of her throat. Amber felt the healing tones. Energy. It was always about energy. Anastasia gave Amber a long look from her place on the other side of Mack and Wheelie.

Minnett didn't jump in to tell her anything, so whatever Anastasia knew or thought, it wasn't terribly important.

Closing her eyes, Amber let herself sink into Mack's physical energetic field. The organs of the cat were different from the organs of a human, but the colors and images translated well for Amber. She worked on sending energy to those areas most in need. Sinking into his spiritual energetic field, Amber was stunned by how cold and sad the place was.

She stood on a hard marble floor that ran as far as she could see. Rain fell from the sky, the sort of rain that you might barely notice for a few minutes but hour after hour, it wears you down. If the image in the realm wasn't bad enough, the pain of loss permeated the place so deeply she thought she now understood the taste of grief.

Amber was consumed with it. She felt the grief entering every cell in her body, washing away any hope she had in life.

"Stop absorbing it and heal him," Minnett ordered. The little tuxedo cat was there, looking ragged and sad in the rain.

Amber sent out healing. She worked on hope, the fact that Drew was alive again, that he'd fought the frost witch. She also sent out as much warm healing energy as she could, hoping to prop up Mack's energetic field. The hope was swallowed up by his sorrow. Even though he knew Drew was alive, the fact that the two were separated caused the big cat pain.

Minnett helped where she could, looking over Amber's shoulder. Back in the physical field, Amber did some more healing.

Pulling out, she had to sit back and cry for a moment.

"*Mack feels badly that you shared his pain,*" Minnett said. "*He didn't want it to intrude on anyone else.*"

"*It's okay,*" Amber sniffed. "*He can't help what he feels. Drew has been very lucky to have such a loyal bond-mate.*"

Amber understood Mack's pain. The hardest part for her had been realizing what she might go through when she lost Minnett. Worse, it might be what Minnett would feel if something happened to Amber.

Wheelie's healing was easier. He wasn't as injured and his psychic field was more positive. He and Cari were still bonded. Amber felt the strength of their connection. She felt him sending magical energy to Cari to help keep her safe.

"*Tell him he can't do that right now,*" Amber said. "*I know it feels necessary but unless they're in the middle of a battle, he doesn't have enough energy to throw it out there.*"

Amber checked physical bodies, using normal medicine, and made sure both cats were warm and comfortable. Minnett and Anastasia stayed with the two guardian cats and purred at them, a light healing and calming spell. Amber noticed it had changed slightly since she'd checked out Mack's psychic field.

Amber was working on Kayley when the young woman was roused by Anastasia's agonized scream.

"What happened?" Kayley asked, sitting up straight, pushing Amber away.

"*Riley is down,*" Minnett said. "*An ice shard once again very close to her heart. The Cat Home creature that was using her body has fled. Riley's vitals are low."*

"I have to go," Amber said, standing up. She noted that Kayley's eyes were slightly unfocused. Her bond-mate, Elmore was feeding her information.

Anson tugged at Amber's pajama bottoms, and she looked down.

"You can't," he said. "It's still snowing. You'll get disoriented. Stay here. The cats can send healing energy to Riley via Anastasia's link. Let Minnett do that. Help her."

Amber studied him. Anson had had internal bleeding. She needed to check on that first. She couldn't let him die.

"I think I'll be fine," Anson said. "Go to Anastasia and lend your strength to her."

Amber hurried back to the cats. Anson was lying. He might not be fine. She ought to save the person who would make it, not go running off to help someone who might die no matter what she did.

Minnett had moved to put a paw on Anastasia's side. Both Mack and Wheelie had curled around the little calico. Amber noted that they were purring a calming spell for her.

Sinking into meditation, Amber linked up with Minnett who pulled healing energy from her to send to Anastasia. So much energy was lost in such a thing, Amber didn't know if it would help from that far away. But else could they do? She didn't want to lose Riley.

Minnett was so closely linked to Anastasia, that Amber nearly watched the entire battle. When the ice golem paused after the last frost witch had been eaten and looked at Courtney, Amber held her breath for a moment before remembering that she had to breathe. She was feeding energy through Anastasia.

Riley was still down, still bleeding, but her energy was more stable than it had been. Amber thought she had a good chance of surviving. She needed to get down to the medic room, clean it up. Everyone had at least small injuries.

And everyone was exhausted. The idea of having to heal them all, the bond-mate cats and their humans, overwhelmed Amber. She didn't have the beds. She didn't have the energy.

Watching through Riley's eyes, the golem leaned over Courtney and took a long sniff. Then it held out its hand. Courtney didn't move. She looked at it.

The golem began to shrink and looked more like Drew, almost like a frost witch wearing Drew's face. Amber wondered if he'd become like Courtney, able to do things with his frost witch. She hoped so, for Mack's sake.

"We wouldn't dare re-bond with him, even so," Minnett said quietly.

Stuart was with Riley and was doing what he could to stabilize her, so both Amber and Minnett pulled out of Anastasia's link.

Amber understood. Re-bonding with Drew would be too dangerous no matter what was found. She took a deep breath, gave Anastasia a long rub, and left her with the other two cats before walking out to the front room to check on Kayley and Anson.

Kayley had tears running down her face. Of course. Elmore had been in the fighting. Amber reached back through the images she'd seen through Riley's eyes. Elmore had a torn ear. It'd be painful as heck, but he wasn't in any real danger.

Amber drew in a breath, trying to steady herself through meditation as Stuart had taught her. Not everyone was as lucky as Elmore.

CHASE

Pain fogged Chase's vision. Everything looked red. Both legs burned as if a fire was eating at them, but they were only aching from the arrow wounds. One leg on the front, which was bleeding through the bandage, and the other had an injury on the back.

Drew had grown and changed while the frost witch had inhabited Chase. The large creature stared down at Courtney, and his former girlfriend looked terrified.

Drew began so shimmer and shrink until he was just a little bigger than he was normally. The big guy looked like he was made of blocks of ice though. That was weird.

Riley lay not far away, barely moving. Stuart had his head bent over her, healing what he could.

Before, even when the frost witch was gone, Chase had been able to sense things. Not now. He couldn't even sense what he normally sensed. He could barely even understand what he was seeing.

Drew moved from Courtney and turned to stand in front of him. He looked Chase up and down.

"You're clear," Drew said. Except it wasn't really his voice. The voice was sort of feminine like the not-Courtney voice Chase had heard in his head but it was a bit rougher as if the edges of the ice blocks cut into the sounds the creature made.

Chase shook his head. If he was still hearing the frost witch, the creature could still influence him.

"No," Drew said. "It's in me. The creature you call a frost witch is gone."

Chase frowned. He had no idea what was going on.

Trag limped up to him and stared at him. No blood marred the pure black fur on the cat, but he had patches of wetness, probably melted snow.

Only then did Chase realize he was sitting in vaguely pinkish water. The ground was churned and messed but he sat in a big puddle. Not deep, but definitely a puddle.

A light breeze blew through the trees, clearing away some of the clouds. Chase thought he even caught a hint of clear night sky.

If the witches weren't gone, they were definitely injured.

Chase drew a deep breath. He realized he was alive.

He'd known that, of course, but he hadn't expected to come out the other side of this battle alive. He'd expected, even hoped, that he'd go through the portal holding onto the frost witch inside him.

"I got it for you," Drew said quietly, as if he could read Chase's mind. Maybe he could.

Drew bent down and sent some healing energy to Chase's legs. It cleared out the fiery pain. Now, the legs just throbbed and pulsed with a deep ache.

"No one here is a healer," Drew apologized. He still sounded a little like the frost witch Chase had had inside him.

The others were leaving Drew alone, though they were

watchful. Tenny's jacket was ripped up one side. She shivered, probably just now noticing she was cold.

Matt held his arm at an awkward angle. His face was pale, though he moved around, looking at others, checking on the cats.

Wilbur meowed softly, breathlessly. Chase turned, which made the pain in his legs flare again. Wilbur was curled near the portal. A long slash of red marred his flank. Spots dribbled from the site of the injury. It didn't seem deep but it was long and likely painful. Between his injury and Matt's, the cat was probably struggling.

Everyone looked as tired as Chase felt.

Drew stood and glanced over at Courtney. She remained pale. Of all of them, she appeared the least injured.

Chase watched, waiting while Drew took one step and then another over to where she waited.

Courtney lifted her chin. Defiant. Ready for whatever happened, though she didn't look as terrified as she had earlier.

Drew's hand reached out. He took Courtney's hand in his. Chase watched her hand disappear into the ice block image of Drew.

Courtney's face hardened and paled. Whatever was happening, it hurt.

Drew pulled back.

Courtney's hand was still there. It looked normal. Nothing out of the ordinary.

Chase watched. She still looked as if she were in pain.

"We are linked," Drew said. At least Chase thought that's what he said.

The portal erupted. A group of creatures that looked human came through, muscles tensed and ready.

Chase closed his eyes, hoping that these creatures were from Cat Home, with their near-human looks, their arms slightly too long, and the clothing that looked like suits out of an old black and white film. All appeared male.

If they weren't from Cat Home, the clowder was in trouble. No one there could stand another fight. Even Courtney looked tired. Only the thing that looked like Drew appeared able to withstand any sort of battle.

With each frost witch that he fed upon, Drew became stronger. He knew more. Part of him reveled in being a god.

"You killed the other because you wouldn't succumb," the shark-dog said. It spoke in words. Its jaw moved, though Drew didn't understand how. Nothing that he saw inside himself was quite real.

"Succumb how?" Drew asked.

"Succumb to power," shark-dog said. "Yes, this is god-like in your world. Not in all worlds. Even in those worlds, you have more power than most. All the power of the frost witches to manifest and change and create as you will exists here. Think of it and you can do it."

Drew knew that was his power now. He was there to destroy if destruction was warranted. He laughed at the shark-dog who seemed confused. The last thing Drew would have named himself was destroyer. But that's what he'd become.

"I'm dead, aren't I?" he asked. "This is the afterlife."

"No." Shark-dog was very certain of that. None of the

others Drew had swallowed appeared around him, though he now knew the things they knew.

This wasn't an afterlife because the creature that had originally been part of what Drew had been swallowed up in had been nearly immortal. His essence was now made up of creatures that had become part of the being he'd taken over within him. Like Frankenstein's monster, he wasn't in one body but many. All of them swallowed whole and their abilities and knowledge merged into one creature.

Maybe a patchwork of spirits was a better description. Not from any one world, but many. Over more eons than Drew could have begun to understand when he was merely human. He understood nuances of the worlds and the portals that he'd never have been able to grasp as a human. His mind was limitless.

He finally understood the importance of his own life, the compassion he brought to the world, and how it spread out from him into the animals, and then into the energy of the earth. Each cat and dog he had offered kindness to let that kindness and love seep threefold into the very molecules of the world around him, making it a better place not just for them but for everything that came in contact with those molecules.

If Drew could weep, he would have. But the construct in which he was held had no tears. As a spirit, he had no tears, but he could feel the emotion even more deeply than he could have as a human. He'd felt Courtney's emotion, the fear of the frost witch which was becoming one with her, making her almost like him but not quite. He'd joined with them so that he'd know if the goodness in Courtney ever lost her battle with the witch.

Drew's thoughts touched Mack. He had to go to his former bond-mate and let him know that he was there. He was fine. Mack would be fine. Drew would heal him.

His need to be with Mack sent him directly to the clowder house, to his former room.

Drew heard Amber in the other room, working on Kayley. He'd have liked to say goodbye to Kayley, too, but that seemed wrong somehow, to say goodbyes so quickly. What he'd become, the ideals that shark-dog fed to him were things he was only beginning to grasp. Kayley, Amber, the rest of them would want to know things he didn't have the vocabulary to explain.

Drew formed a hand. Anastasia hissed softly.

The hand touched Mack lightly. Drew reformed the bond for just a moment. Normally, that would have been Mack's choice. Now, he had the power.

"*Be well,*" Drew whispered, telepathically only to Mack. Even Grey and the other creatures from Cat Home wouldn't hear his words. "*I'm okay. I'll come if you need me.*"

"*Don't leave,*" Mack pleaded. Drew felt the pain slowly falling away from the cat. Both the emotional pain of loss and the pain of his injuries. Drew understood that he'd thrown himself into the fray in hopes of dying. He didn't want to live without his bond-mate.

"*There's more than we ever dreamed,*" Drew said. "*I can't take you. It's wrong, somehow, for what I am, for what my existence requires of me now. But I'm here. And I'm glad you were my bond-mate.*"

Mack settled in, saying nothing, feeding him images of their life together from the moment they'd met at the shelter and Mack had felt Drew, felt all of who he was, and had chosen him. He relived their best moments in an instant of time.

When Mack stretched, flexing his body in a way he couldn't have moments ago, Drew withdrew. Once more, he was back near the portal. No one looked at him or noticed him. While he could have sent himself anywhere in the worlds, the portals were easier.

Drew stepped through this portal to a place that was drawing him. The threat there wasn't a frost witch but it was magical, and he was needed. When the portal closed behind him and he stepped onto a new world, the link to Courtney tied him to his birth world and through her, his link to Mack, thin and ephemeral but there all the same.

The link was no longer telepathic, but he knew the cat continued to rest, and that knowledge set Drew's mind at ease. He wasn't forever separated from his bond-mate.

STUART

Stuart tried to remember the return to the clowder house but it eluded him even a day later. The place was crowded with Cat Home representatives, himself, Courtney, and the regular clowder. Drew was gone. Stuart knew, deep down, that Mack's former bond-mate wasn't coming back.

Trag and Stuart had un-bonded. Chances were, Trag would re-bond with Chase.

Riley rested in her own bed, healing. One of the Cat Home beings was adept at healing. Riley swore her hips felt better than they had in years.

Once she heard how much better Riley felt, Amber had insisted upon being taught some of the healing techniques.

Looking out his window, Stuart noted that the snow was mostly gone, even just a day later. One advantage of having the worst room, no one wanted to share with him. Tenny and Kayley were sharing a room so that someone from Cat Home could use Tenny's room.

Fin and Anson were rooming together upstairs in Fin's

room. Again, someone from Cat Home was using Anson's space.

Base Command had called multiple times, talking to Stuart, giving him orders. Darla wanted him to bring Grey, or someone, the emphasis on someone, to Base Command so they could thank them personally.

Stuart had no plan to take anyone who didn't volunteer.

A tap at the door made him turn from the window. It was late in the day already.

"Yes?" he called.

Courtney opened the door. Stuart noticed the stance. Confident rather than shy and uncertain. Not just shyly proud of what she'd done, not surprised by her power any longer. Now she owned it. Held it.

"I think I'm going to drive home," she said. "Even if we haven't gotten rid of all the witches and they come through again, Dawn and I should be good alone."

Stuart nodded. "Will you go back to work at the clinic?" He couldn't quite see Courtney working in a medical clinic collecting funds from insurance companies any longer. She wasn't that girl.

"I doubt it," Courtney said. "I've got some money from Base Command for my "service" as they call it and I'm on a list that offers me some money each month. You know, just in case I'm needed. I'll figure out what Dawn and I are good at soon enough."

Stuart nodded. "I'm glad. I'm glad you're finding your feet."

Courtney looked down at her feet as if she were taking him literally. Stuart hid a smile. He might associate the words and actions, but she was pensive. As if suddenly she wasn't confident.

Looking up she smiled a little, but wouldn't meet his eyes.

"Can I contact you? You know, like visit or get a phone number. No one else really understands me."

"I'm not sure I do," Stuart admitted.

"But you're like me, sort of. I mean, not completely human anymore. The people here know what happened, but it didn't happen to them. They get the magic and the weirdness and we'll always be friends, because even other clowders aren't going to be able to completely understand what happened here, but they're still human. When their bondmates die, they'll go back to their lives, mostly," Courtney said.

Stuart nodded, finally understanding. She needed someone like her. Someone to let her know she wasn't alone. He might not get what had happened to her, but she'd understood how alone he felt as he changed and became less human. She was on her own path to not being human. Maybe he could help before he became too much like Grey and the others.

"You can always call me."

"And if you need me… I don't know… maybe to remind you how human you still are, you can call me, too," Courtney said.

"Grey told me I don't have to go back to Base Command. He's gotten that I don't feel as if I fit in there—that I regret what I started. I can live where I want, though I'll be asked to go back to Base Command when I no longer fit in outside," Stuart said. "Grey actually apologized for the fact that I've changed and have no choice about the decision. I think they'll be changing how they chose people to work at Base Command from now on."

It had seemed uncommonly human of him. Of course, Grey had been stuck in their world for longer than the others. Perhaps the worlds did influence the beings from Cat

Home, at least in their ability to understand the tiny creatures that inhabited the other worlds.

"I'll know who to call if I think I need help when Base Command calls, then," Courtney said. "I need to go down and start saying good-bye. I've done what healing I can, although I'm glad Uriah was here to do the heavy lifting. I'm not sure just pouring energy in would have helped."

Stuart smiled and watched as she left. It felt a little scary to be untethered from Base Command, though he was still part of it, would still have to answer to Darla, at least from a distance. He didn't know where he'd live, though he was thinking of going back to his childhood home of Florida. He could be like Drew and volunteer in a shelter. Cats, even ordinary cats, liked him.

Knowing he was in contact with Courtney would help. There'd be one person who wasn't Base Command that would potentially outlive him. He'd never realized what a comforting thought that was. While she might be leaving, Stuart had to spend at least a few more days at the clowder to help them get back to full strength. He even had a shift at portal watch later that evening.

COURTNEY

I t took Courtney two days to say her goodbyes to the clowder. It wasn't like she was moving across the country. She was going back to her little house which was only half-hour or an hour across town depending upon traffic and the route taken.

After making sure she would keep in contact with Stuart, she'd started talking to everyone, letting them know she planned to leave. It had gotten dark, they'd eaten a heavy meal and Courtney had been too exhausted to drive. The next day, she'd helped the clowder rearrange furniture and make decisions on the places that needed to be redecorated.

They'd even put the tree back up, though it was much the worse for wear. Still, it was theirs. The broken and bent branches seemed to symbolize their many wounds.

All the Cat Home Representatives except Grey started on their return journey. They weren't going through the local portal but one in South Africa. They'd get there a few days before they needed to leave and check on that clowder. She felt the non-humans moving around the world. Yet another new sensation.

She had a lot to get used to. And she had to make sure she used whatever powers she had to help others. Drew had been very clear that he would come for her if she used them selfishly. She sensed him, too, a distant presence on the edge of her mind. Their connection stretched and played like a fishing line as the worlds he jumped to moved further or closer to her own.

Courtney had no desire to step through a portal, ever. She had changed enough as it was. Now she needed to figure out what it was she wanted to do.

Like a five-year-old thinking about what she wanted to be as a grown-up, Courtney understood she could do pretty much anything she wanted.

She didn't want to rely on her power to get what she wanted, even if she didn't need to worry about being selfish. She wanted to live her life on her own merit. Even if she wasn't really Courtney anymore, but Courtney Dawn, she wanted to do it on the merits they both had.

Dawn's interest had run to building things and understanding how they worked. Courtney's dad was going to be shocked at the things his daughter had learned over the holidays.

Courtney had already determined she'd spend Christmas Day at the clowder house. She'd go to her family on Christmas Eve.

Saying good-bye to Chase had been weird. He and Trag weren't yet re-bonded, but Trag was hanging out in Chase's room again. Chase and Courtney would always be exes. There wasn't any chance of getting back together.

Courtney didn't understand what he'd done while possesssed by the frost witch. She knew Chase didn't understand what she'd done. They'd each made choices and each had lived through it, though Chase had killed one of his friends and nearly killed his friend's bond-mate cat. He'd hurt Trag. In fact, without Courtney, the clowder might have had more fatalities.

His choices hadn't worked, though they'd worked out for him in the end, largely thanks to Drew. Drew was clearly a better person than Courtney would ever be. Perhaps that was why he'd been the one subsumed into the creature that came after the frost witches.

Courtney considered putting up a few Christmas decorations when she returned home but decided against it. Christmas meant nothing to Dawn. Courtney had people to see. Dawn found people fascinating. And the neighborhood had fresh energy. Lots of it.

Her folks' older house would have different energy, life force energy that had seeped into the walls. Dawn was going to have a feast on that, too. And there would be people there to sip from here and there for even more energy.

Vampire shows no longer interested her. Living the life of a creature so similar to them meant such fiction wasn't for her. Not vegging in front of the television would give her more time to learn what it was that really interested her.

Next door, her neighbor was considering having pizza for dinner. Courtney didn't know how she knew, but she did. Dawn's latent telepathic abilities let her hear thoughts from time to time. Stuart had talked about being able to do that.

Maybe Courtney could become a detective. Imagine if she could read minds while interviewing people! Courtney chuckled to herself before calling for her own pizza. The food had sounded good. Even Dawn agreed.

Courtney liked that Dawn liked her little house. Maybe it hadn't been such a bad thing that she'd let her father bully her into buying this house instead of a condo. With her abilities now, having a house was probably a good thing. And if monsters or killers were coming after her, they'd better watch out.

Courtney Dawn was the one *they* should fear.

ABOUT BONNIE ELIZABETH

Bonnie Elizabeth could never decide what to do, so she wrote stories about amazing things and sometimes she even finished them.

While rejection stung her so badly in person, she spent most of her young life talking to cats and dogs rather than people, she was unusually resilient when it came to rejections on her writing, racking up a good number of them.

Floating through a variety of jobs, including veterinary receptionist, cemetery administrator, and finally acupuncturist, she continued to write stories.

When the internet came along (yes she's old), she started blogging as her cat, because we all know cats don't notice rejection. Then she started publishing.

Bonnie writes in a variety of genres. Her popular Whisper series is contemporary fantasy and her Teenage Fairy Godmother series is written for teens. She has been published in a number of anthologies and is working on expanding her writing repertoire.

She lives with her husband (who talks less than she does) and her three cats, who always talk back.

Stay in Touch

ALSO BY BONNIE ELIZABETH

THE FROST WITCH SAGA

October Snow

November Frost

December Storm

APPALACHIAN SOULS

Souls Lost

Souls Broken

THE ASH JERICHO SERIES

An Inheritance to Die For

A Discovery to Die For

A Distraction to Die For

THE WHISPER NOVELS

Whisper Bound

Taken by the Sound

An Air of Suspicion

Little Dog Lost

Death Interrupted

Down in Whisper

A Haunting Whisper

A Haunting Attraction

Secrets Not Whispers

Only Human

OTHER NOVELS

Ghosts from the Past

Unnatural Secrets

Find them all at your favorite bookseller or check us out at
MyBigFatOrangeCat.com